NEKOMAH CREEK
·:·CHRISTMAS·:·

Other books by Linda Crew

for children

NEKOMAH CREEK

SOMEDAY I'LL LAUGH ABOUT THIS

CHILDREN OF THE RIVER

for adults

ORDINARY MIRACLES

NEKOMAH CREEK ·CHRISTMAS·

by

Linda Crew

Illustrated by Charles Robinson

DELACORTE PRESS   NEW YORK

Published by
Delacorte Press
Bantam Doubleday Dell Publishing Group, Inc.
1540 Broadway
New York, New York 10036

Library of Congress Cataloging in Publication Data

Crew, Linda.
    Nekomah Creek Christmas / by Linda Crew ; illustrated by
Charles Robinson.
        p.   cm.
    Companion to: Nekomah Creek.
    Summary: Robby and his boisterous family spend the Christmas
season preparing for Robby's reluctant debut in the school play
and his parents' income tax audit.
    ISBN 0-385-32047-7
    [1. Christmas—Fiction. 2. Plays—Fiction. 3. Schools—
Fiction. 4. Family life—Fiction. 5. Oregon—Fiction.]
I. Robinson, Charles, ill. II. Title.
PZ7.C86815Ng 1994
[Fic]—dc20   94-478 CIP AC

Manufactured in the United States of America

November 1994

10 9 8 7 6 5 4 3 2 1

BVG

*For Mary and William
and, at their insistence,
for Buddy Wabbit*

With special thanks to
Gail Gerdemann

CONTENTS

No We Don't!

"Oh, I just *love* theater," my mom said, turning to Dad. "Don't you?"

Behind the wheel of the minivan, Dad checked left and right before pulling out from Nekomah Creek Road onto the coast highway. "Beth," he said, "this is a kiddie Thanksgiving pageant we're heading for, not the Oregon Shakespearean Festival."

"Okay!" Mom laughed. "So I'm desperate."

She always talks about all the great plays she used to go to back when she lived up in Seattle. Not much like that going on around Nekomah Creek. Or even Douglas Bay, the nearest real town.

"Still," she went on, "that exciting opening night feeling is always the same, I don't care if it's Broadway or Presbyterian Preschool."

Well, I'm sorry, but personally I just couldn't get that whipped up. I had even suggested being left home. I thought I was old enough to handle it now.

Horrified, Mom and Dad had shushed me.

"Freddie and Lucy are counting on you being there, Robby," Mom said. "Don't you dare hurt their feelings."

So here I was, riding along on the rain-slickened road over the head to Douglas Bay, wishing I was home by the wood stove with a book.

Mom twisted around in her seat to look at me. "Think you'll try out for the school Christmas play?"

I sighed. She'd been dropping hints ever since she saw a note about auditions in the school newsletter, and it didn't take a rocket scientist to figure out what the right answer was as far as she was concerned. But I just shrugged without looking up from my paperback.

"Oh, sweetie," she said. "Can you actually read in the car? Doesn't it make you sick?"

Now what can I say to this? Yes, I am apparently able to read in the car. If it made me sick, wouldn't I quit? What she really means is, *she* can't read in a car.

"Have you got enough light?"

"Ye-es." I wiggled my trusty penlight.

"Well, anyway, you'd be so good in a play. Wouldn't he, Bill? He's got a mind like a steel trap. He could memorize lines"—she snapped her fingers— "like that!"

So what? Being able to memorize lines doesn't necessarily make a person eager to terrify himself by getting up in front of a lot of people to prove it.

From the seat behind me, three-year-old Freddie and Lucy were chanting, "No we don't! No we don't!"

"The twins've got *their* lines nailed anyway," Dad said.

"No we don't! No we don't!" This had been going

on for days. What could "No we don't" have to do with Thanksgiving? By now I was extremely curious and extremely sick of it.

I snapped my head around. "Will you two please stop kicking the seat?"

"Land ho!" Freddie shouted.

Okay, now *that* line I could guess.

"Land home!" Lucy cried.

"No, *I* say dat!" Freddie warned her.

"Dad," I pleaded, "make 'em quit kicking." I turned and sliced my penlight across them with a light-saber sound. *Vruum.*

Lucy shrieked.

"Kids, kids," Mom said.

"No we don't! No we don't!"

Giving up on my book, I sank down and stuck my fingers in my ears. Weren't two enthusiastic actors more than enough for one family? Why was Mom so eager to put me onstage too? Then I thought of something. I sat up and leaned forward, gripping the back of her seat.

"The thing is, Mom, they want each kid's mother to sew his costume. You're always saying how you don't have enough time for stuff and you're way behind . . ."

"But Robby, this is something I'd *make* time for. I *love* doing costumes. You know that."

"Oh. Yeah." I sank back. "Right."

"Being in plays is so much fun," she said, and then she started in about how lucky our school was to have such a neat stage.

Give it up, I was thinking. Nothing could change my mind.

When she finally paused for breath, Dad turned on one of his jazzy Cajun music tapes and we blasted ourselves with that until we pulled into the parking lot.

Now, for a school at a church, the preschool wasn't very churchy. When I went there, they never talked about God or Jesus or anything. Nothing but the quick thanks-for-the-graham-cracker grace.

Mom said this was what you call an "outreach" program, something that showed people the church was a friendly place and helped draw people there.

I guess it worked on us, because we started going every Christmas Eve. And then some regular Sundays too. Finally, last year, Lucy, Freddie, and I found ourselves standing in front of the congregation in the company of a couple of babies in long dresses, getting water sprinkled on our heads. I was probably setting some kind of record for oldest kid ever to get baptized in that church.

Outreach. I pictured some big old hand rising up out of the church and sort of sweeping us in.

Now we took Freddie and Lucy into their classroom, where all the kids were being hustled into their construction-paper Pilgrim hats and collars.

"Break a leg!" Mom said, stooping to tie Lucy's bonnet. She'd already explained that was theater talk for "Good luck!"

From beneath his black, buckled hat, Freddie gave me a stern look. "Robby, you watch me on the stage."

"Right, Freddie." I mean, what else would there be to do? He can be so bossy.

Mom pulled both of them close and whispered in their ears—probably some final advice against nose picking or pulling up T-shirts to show off tummies while onstage.

Then we left them and headed down the hall. All these little guys milling around at the classroom doors made me feel so huge. I even felt big compared to the other older brothers and sisters who'd come along. Most of them looked about six or seven, but I turned seven before Freddie and Lucy were even born.

We followed the crowd into this room they call Education Hall. What a zoo—everybody jostling around, trying to get the best seats. There must have been six people for each preschooler—parents, grandparents, brothers, and sisters—and the room steamed with a couple hundred damp rain parkas packed together in the warmth.

"Look at all the video cameras," I said. "I don't believe it."

First the school people made some announcements, but you could hardly hear because the audience was so restless and excited. They might as well have started a chant: "We. Want. The kids!"

Finally Lucy and Freddie shuffled out onto the stage with the other three-year-old Pilgrims. The parents went "Aaww!"

Ever notice how people go berserk over little guys? They *are* pretty cute, I guess. Sometimes I forget that because I'm just so busy living in the middle of the ones we've got.

For the first couple of years, Freddie and Lucy were nothing but funny, squally babies. They took up a lot of Mom and Dad's time, but you couldn't really get *mad* at them. Lately they'd been turning into real people, though. Stubborn people. With opinions. When

you're arguing with someone, you don't think much about their cuteness.

But now, seeing them up on the stage with the others, I felt sort of proud. Hey, that's my baby brother, the littlest guy. And that's my sister, the one in the panda T-shirt!

Mom and Dad were just grinning away. Let's face it, Lucy and Freddie are their little darlings.

Suddenly I got a weird feeling, like I wished *I* was one of those Pilgrims. But I was ten. I was never going to be cute in that "Aw, gee" way again.

Dads hoisted video cameras to their shoulders. Moms squinted into viewfinders. Bulbs flashed.

Freddie spotted us and arced his whole arm windshield-wiper style, while Lucy kept her elbow pressed to her side, wiggling her fingers at us from her hip. We all made a big deal out of waving back, although I did feel sort of embarrassed.

Finally the teacher began reading from her script. "A long time ago some people lived in England," she said, "a land across the sea."

A bigger kid, probably from the four-year-old class, strutted out in a glittered crown and tablecloth cape and climbed to stand on a table. He looked at the teacher, who nodded.

Scowling, he drew himself up and pointed at the kids below. "You have to go to my church!"

The Pilgrims all sucked in a big breath, glancing at each other to make sure they had actually arrived at the long-awaited moment. Yes! This was it!

They reared back. "No we don't!" they bellowed.

Mom, Dad, and I grinned at each other.

"Oh yes you do!" the king argued.

"NO WE DON'T!" the Pilgrims shouted even louder, barely getting it out before breaking up in giggles.

The Pilgrim leader stepped forward. "Come on, guys, we'll go to America! There we can go to whatever church we want!"

They shuffled a cardboard boat across the stage. The king shook his fist at them. I saw Freddie do a nyeah-nyeah right back. Then the Pilgrims all had a great time pretending to be seasick, throwing up over the sides.

Finally Freddie looked up and got the nod from his teacher.

I nudged Mom and whispered, "This must be the 'Land ho!' part."

Freddie leaned to the right and shaded his eyes with his hand. But he didn't say "Land ho!"

"Yo!" he yelled. "Yo! Land!"

The audience laughed. They loved him.

Mom beamed. I'll bet she was already picturing Freddie accepting his Academy Award, thanking his mother for supporting his theatrical ambitions from the very beginning.

After the Pilgrims crash-landed on Plymouth Rock (a couple fell out and waded ashore), the teacher told what a tough time they had that first winter and mentioned that some even died. Apparently Lucy had volunteered to be one of the goners. She fell down and stuck her legs straight up in the air.

"Now I'm glad she wouldn't wear a dress," Mom whispered.

Later, after the Indians in brown grocery-sack vests came out and showed the Pilgrims what was what, I noticed Lucy jumped back up and got in on the feast with the rest of them.

It was all pretty funny until the end, when the kids held hands, got serious, and sang a churchy song with a chorus of "We are truly thankful." No big deal, really, but the way they were all lined up there, just singing their little hearts out about how great the world is . . . Well, I heard this sniffing and when I peeked over, sure enough, Mom's eyes were leaking makeup.

The hymn ended to thunderous applause.

"Good job," we were still telling the twins as Mom and Dad strapped them back into their car seats.

"Yo!" Freddie said for the twentieth time. "Yo! Land!"

"He has definitely got the bug," Mom said.

I was glad I'd gone. The play was short and sweet and a lot more yuks than I'd expected. Also, the trail mix snack we got afterward had an excellent ratio of M&M's to Cheerios!

Still, there was a little something nagging at me. As we drove home, I was trying to remember: when was the last time Mom had gotten that glowy look about anything *I'd* done?

∴ 2 ∴

Gloomy News

Nekomah Creek and the narrow road twist along together up the little valley where we live, and at our five acres, the driveway starts with a plank bridge over the gurgling water.

When I pedaled my bike over it after school the next day, I found Dad on a ladder, stringing Christmas lights along the front porch of the house.

"Give me a hand," he said. "Maybe we could get this eave finished before *Mister Rogers* wraps up and the kids come climbing after me."

"Sure, Dad."

It wasn't unusual to find him home like this—his work is right out in the wood shop, making storm windows for people. When he has time for it, that is. Mostly he's busy taking care of Freddie and Lucy.

I leaned my bike against the porch and took off my helmet. "Can we do the two big trees by the road this year? You *are* going to buy more lights, aren't you?"

"Of course!" Dad makes a point of adding at least one new string every Christmas. Mom says he'll end up having to specify in his will who'll get the lights collection, because at this rate, it'll be worth thousands someday!

She kids him, but I think it's great. I mean, Ben Hammond's dad is nice, but Ben says he acts like decorating for Christmas is just one more farm chore. And West Feikart's dad thinks electric lights for decoration are a waste of power. He worries because the electricity comes from the dams that stop the rivers and keep the salmon from spawning. Well, that's true, I guess, and sure something to think about, but there are lots of electrical things I'd do without before I'd give up the sight of our house on a dark December night, outlined in jewels of blue, red, and green, a make-believe electric candle glowing in each window.

We *need* these lights. Around here this time of year there are only about three colors: green, brown, and gray. It gets gloomy. The last of the flaming vine maple in the woods is gone, and Dad's vegetable garden —so full of color two months before—is a soggy, mucky mess. He says it's no accident they started celebrating Christmas at just the season when folks in the northern parts most needed something to perk them up.

Handing the end of a new string up to Dad, I heard the squeak and bump of our old blue pickup on the plank bridge. It was Mom, home from her part-time job at Douglas Bay Graphics. Now, I'm sorry to say that she is not as enthusiastic as the rest of us about the way Dad gets carried away over holidays, so it didn't surprise me one bit when, right after she got out and gave us a "Hi, guys," she looked up at Dad on the ladder, crossed her arms over her chest, and heaved this big sigh.

"Bill, these are Christmas lights."

He squinted closely at one of the bulbs. "Well, I'll be darned."

"And tomorrow's Thanksgiving."

"Ha! Can't fool me on *that* one. The turkey's thawing even as we speak!"

She sighed again. "I thought we agreed the day *after* Thanksgiving was the earliest any Christmas decorations ought to go up."

"Oh, was it *after*?" He winked at me. "Silly me. I thought it was the day *before*!"

"Bill!"

"Hey, I'm just doing like it says in the Bible."

"Huh?"

"Yeah, right there in the beginning. *Let there be lights!*"

Mom rolled her eyes. "The decorations from your birthday party haven't been cleaned up yet. Everything's always overlapping."

"What's wrong with that?" I said. I *liked* the idea of one holiday running into the next.

"I can't keep up, that's what! You guys are always racing ahead to the next thing while I'm still trying to shovel out from the last."

"Come on, Beth." Dad climbed down the ladder. "Robby and I'll put the lights up and we'll take them down, too."

"By Valentine's Day?"

"Hey, I got the rotten jack-o'-lanterns off the driveway today. And you didn't even notice."

"Well . . ." she said, giving in to his hug. "I guess I should be grateful it's just lights." She peered up at him. "It *is* just going to be lights, right?"

The year before, Dad had found a bunch of big advertising cutouts at the dump—a snowman, a Santa with reindeer, and a gingerbread house. He hauled them home and set them up with lights out by our bridge. It looked really cool, and lots of people were driving their kids up here to check it out. So many, in fact, that some of the neighbors started complaining about the traffic, and two cars went in the ditch trying to turn around. I knew Mom didn't want to go through that again.

"Mom!" Freddie and Lucy came banging out onto the porch, fighting their way into the middle of Mom and Dad's hug.

"Whoa," I said. "Nice hairdo, Lucy."

It had taken my little sister the longest time to grow any hair beyond a few blond wisps, and at the moment, what she had was sticking up in separate clumps, each held by a different colored hair clip.

"Sank you," Dad said in a silly French accent, swooping around Lucy, fluffing her tufts as she grinned. "I call zis style zee Funny-do. All zee fashionable ladies vill be vanting it."

"Anything good in the mail?" Mom asked.

"Oh, I forgot to check." He climbed the ladder again. "Kind of got involved with other stuff."

Freddie's face lit up. "Maybe the ants came!"

We had given Dad an ant farm for his birthday. Then it turned out you had to send away to some company and they'd ship the ants.

"Freddie," I said, "we only mailed the coupon a

couple of days ago." This is one of those hard facts of life the little guys haven't learned yet: If you send for something, it will take forever to come.

Mom headed down the long gravel drive to the mailbox, the twins racing ahead of her.

"Don't run into the road!" she yelled.

When she came back up a few minutes later she was practically staggering. Dad and I could both tell something was wrong.

Dad climbed down the ladder. "What is it, Hon?"

"Galaxy Greetings," she wailed, dropping the rest of the mail on the porch step. "The whole deal is off. The market's not right or something."

Oh, no. Mom had been so excited about this company wanting to make cards out of her miniature paintings. She's an artist, see, and she does these neat little pen-and-ink and watercolor pictures of flowers and sometimes funny things like vegetable people hanging out their laundry. The greeting cards were the reason she'd felt she could afford to work at home more and only go into her other job a couple of days a week.

"Bummer, Mom." I picked up the bundle of mail.

Dad put his arm around her. She looked like she wanted to cry.

"It must be a dumb company, Mom. If they can't see what great cards your paintings would make . . ."

"Thanks, Robby," Mom said.

I turned away from her sad face and thumbed through the rest of the letters. "The Internal Revenue Service," I read.

Mom's head snapped up. "What? I missed that." She took the envelope and tore it open. "Oh, great.

We're going to be audited." She sagged against the porch post. "I don't believe this—two pieces of rotten news in one day."

"What's 'audited'?" I asked.

Dad took the IRS letter. "December nineteenth. Can they *do* that? Come for an audit so close to Christmas?"

"It *is* awfully short notice," Mom said.

"Uh, well, actually," Dad said, "I guess they did phone about this a few weeks ago."

"What?" She straightened up. "And you didn't *tell* me?"

"Hey, I just figured, why upset you?"

"Oh, Bill, don't you realize what this means?"

"*I* don't realize what this means," I said. "Would somebody mind explaining?"

"An audit is to check how you figured your income taxes," Dad said, "and make sure you didn't cheat."

"Dad! You wouldn't cheat."

"Of course not. And nobody's saying we did. The agent assured me this is just random bad luck on our part. They spot-check a few families every year to see if people are being honest."

"Oh, this is great," Mom said. "They'll want to see a receipt for every tube of watercolor paint I've bought, and all Daddy's records for his storm window business." She turned to Dad. "This would have been much easier back when we were teaching and just filed those forms from the school district. Now we'll have to dig out a whole year's worth of papers—all those shoe boxes full of bills and cancelled checks."

I knew the ones she meant. They were all crammed

into the guest room closet, the one she always warned us to stay out of.

"It's true," Dad said, "that I probably haven't been as organized about it as I should have."

Don't you hate it when parents get upset? Even if you're feeling okay yourself, it seems rude to be cheerful when they've got big problems.

"And no ants," Lucy said, getting into the spirit of gloom.

Mom put her hands on her hips. "Bill," she said, "if an agent of the Internal Revenue Service is coming to this house, the last thing you ought to be doing is hanging Christmas lights."

"Don't worry, Honey, I'll take care of everything. And Thanksgiving's all under control. Low key, right? And no company, so—"

"Oh, no!" Mom took a sharp breath. "I just thought of something. Your brother's coming on the twentieth of December, right? What if the auditor's still here?"

"Which brother?" I asked, because my dad has four.

"Uncle Fred and Aunt Pat," Mom told me. "They're bringing the kids up for Christmas. We weren't going to tell you in case it didn't work out."

Cameron and Cassandra, my California cousins. Make that three bits of bad news.

Well, four, if you count the ants.

·: 3 :·

A Cry on the Wind

"I already know one thing I want for Christmas," I told my mom on Saturday morning. Lucy and Freddie and I were gobbling Swedish pancakes in the kitchen.

"Oh?" Mom said. "What's that?"

"These." I held up a magazine ad for a certain brand of high-top running shoes.

Mom frowned at the glossy picture. "Aren't those the incredibly expensive kind?"

"Not the *very* most expensive," I said. "And Jesse has them."

Spatula poised in midair, she cocked her head. "Is that so."

Jesse Glenn's my new friend who moved here this year from Massachusetts. He wears cool shoes and T-shirts from interesting places none of the rest of us have ever been. And I don't mean Disney World Mickey Mouse shirts, either. I'm talking about brainy gray shirts from the Smithsonian or the American Museum of Natural History in New York City.

"We'll have to watch it moneywise this Christmas," Mom reminded me, "with my greeting card deal falling through."

"Oh, right." Darn that Galaxy Greetings! Thanks to them, Mom was all bummed out, and that made it gloomy for us too.

"Ta da!" Dad strutted in, dangling an orange plastic Forest Service tag. "Our official Christmas tree cutting permit!"

"Yay!" I burst out, and the twins joined me, cheering for Christmas trees even if they didn't have a clue about permits.

"Oh, no you don't," Mom said, tossing her curly ponytail back. "No tree until we make some progress on the tax mess." She got Lucy in a headlock and gave her syrupy face a swipe with a washcloth. "Besides, it's not even December yet."

I groaned. I am all for having the Christmas tree up as long as possible.

"Pancakes, Bill?"

"Sure," Dad said, playing it safe. Mom's very proud of her pancakes because, other than cookies, they're about the only thing she knows how to make. If we don't eat them, her feelings get hurt.

After she dished up Dad's, she went to the coat closet and pulled down a sack of rental video cassettes. "You guys can watch these while we tackle the taxes."

My folks don't like us to watch too much TV, but every once in a while when they're desperate to have the twins distracted, we get to have a video orgy.

When we'd finished eating and the sticky dishes were stacked in the sink, Mom popped the first tape in the machine. "Now, try not to bother Daddy and me unless it's an emergency, okay?" Then she headed upstairs.

Dad gave us a sad thumbs up and followed her.

The video store in Douglas Bay isn't all that big, so we tend to get our same favorite movies over and over again. This one was about a family that moves to the wilderness and has so many bad things happen all at once it's sort of funny.

We got busy taking the two sofas apart to make a log cabin.

"Robby get down the high bwankets," Lucy said, dragging me toward the linen closet, and Freddie started gathering the stuffed animals. I passed out the flashlights and we stocked the "cabin" with boxes of crackers; Dad's homegrown, roasted pumpkin seeds; and a package of baloney.

By the time the dad in the story got attacked by the cougar, we had most of the furniture piled in a heap and we were jumping around on everything in the darkened room, waving flashlights. I'm probably too old to do this with kids my own age, but with my little brother and sister somehow it feels different.

When Mom came down, she took one look and shut her eyes. "I *wish* I hadn't seen this."

Hey, at least we weren't lying around like couch potatoes. This was *active* TV viewing.

On her way back up with a coffee mug in each hand she paused, drawn by the part of the movie where the mom gets delirious with fever and the kids are screaming because a bear's trying to break in. Lucy and Freddie screamed right along.

"Guess I shouldn't complain," Mom said. "That bear makes an IRS official look pretty tame."

"Wait, Mom," I warned as she headed up the stairs again, "you're going to miss the good part. Pretty soon's where the dad gets caught in the avalanche."

"Yes, well, I have to rescue *your* father from *his* avalanche."

"Huh?"

"When we opened that closet, six years worth of papers fell out on him."

"Really? Come on! Let's go see!"

"No, no, now you all stay down here. We're just starting to get it sorted out."

After the movie family's happy ending, I put on our favorite Christmas tape. It has a great old cartoon about Santa and his elves and a lot of dancing, singing toys, all done opera style. When it came to the part where Santa gets in his sleigh to take off for deliveries, Dad appeared on the landing and joined him in a booming voice:

"Fare-WELLL . . . my merry little elves . . . Farewell! Farewell! Farewell!" He marched down the stairs singing, one hand over his chest, the other held out like one of those dramatic Italian guys.

"Bill!" I heard Mom call. "We're not stopping yet, are we?"

Dad posed for us and sang back up the stairs. "I NEEEED a break, my darling wife . . . A break! A break! A break . . . !"

The twins cheered, "Daddy! Daddy!" snapping the

opera spell, turning him back into plain old silly Dad.

"Yoika doo!" He vaulted the banister and dove into the pile of cushions and blankets and crunching crackers. Then he turned over and sighed with satisfaction. "Ah, this looks like the perfect spot."

We all jumped on him, wrestling around until somebody accidentally got bonked hard enough to cry. Then we watched the Santa cartoon a few more times until everybody knew most of the words. "Fare-WELLL . . . my merry little elves . . ."

I forget what we did after that, but I'm pretty sure Dad never did get back upstairs to the tax papers.

The next day we got hauled off to church. Mom said a couple of hours of enforced civilized behavior would be good for everybody, especially her.

Well, I'll be honest. Church can be pretty boring. Sometimes it's so dull there is nothing to do but listen to the minister and try to figure out what he's saying. One time I gave one of my interpretations to my folks. "I think he was saying that we people are sort of rotten sometimes, but we're asking God to help us out anyway."

"Ha! That's pretty good, Robby," Dad said. "That about sums it up."

What I didn't get was, why couldn't the *minister* sum it up? He took half an hour to say that.

Today I figured his message was something like this: *Loving each other is more important than anything else.* Okay, except as you might have noticed, that's the sort of thing that can seem perfectly clear when you're sitting in church, but gets fuzzier once you're

outside. The minute I find myself in trouble for a squabble Freddie has started, for example, proving I'm right suddenly seems more important than brotherly love.

"The choir was really something today," Mom said as we drove home over Tillicum Head. "Especially that last hymn."

No kidding. I'm never bored during the singing. A thunderous organ and fifty voices soaring into let-all-the-stops-out harmony . . . This is music you don't just hear—you actually feel it vibrating right up through you. Makes my chest quiver to where I'm scared I'll cry. *Awesome,* I guess is the word. What *awesome* meant before it got tacked on to everything from shoes to pizza, that is.

"You know, Bill," Mom said. "It's too bad we can't get you involved in the music program at church."

"Oh, right. My accordion and I would fit right in."

"You wouldn't have to play that. You could play anything, I bet." Mom turned to us. "Your dad has an amazing amount of musical talent."

It was true. We'd given him the accordion for his birthday just a few weeks before and he had already taught himself to play it.

"It's such a shame," Mom said, "to hide your light under a bushel."

Dad shrugged. "Some of us just aren't performers." He winked at me. "Some of us *like* hanging out under bushels."

At home we took off our church clothes and ate sandwiches made from the last of the Thanksgiving turkey. Then Mom and Dad headed upstairs to work on the taxes while we turned on the videos and started arguing. Freddie didn't want to watch anything but the Santa opera cartoon. He just loved marching around singing Santa's lines, but Lucy was fed up with having to be his audience.

After a while, Mom came out on the second floor balcony. "Will you stop this bickering?"

Everybody clamored to tell their side of it until Mom put her hands over her ears and shut her eyes. When we were all quiet, we heard a sound in the background—Dad's accordion.

"Bill!" Mom whirled and marched back to the guest room.

When I looked out the window in the middle of the afternoon, the sun was sparkling on raindrops that quivered from every twig and fir needle. It looked good out there, and cool. The house suddenly seemed hot and stuffy.

"Can't we go get the tree?" I asked Mom and Dad from the guest room door. "This is the first time it's stopped raining in days."

Dad rose from the card table they'd set up and pulled aside the window curtain. "He's got a point, Beth."

Downstairs, Freddie and Lucy were screaming bloody murder at each other again.

"Oh, all right," Mom said, heading down to break up the fight. Under her breath she was muttering this morning's hymn. *Grant us wisdom, grant us courage* . . . And then that line she likes about stopping thy children's warring madness . . .

After the usual thirty-minute rubber-boot roundup, we were all crammed into the pickup, the kids hyper over getting to ride without car seats. Mom and Dad are usually strict about that, but we needed the truck bed for the tree, and the cab part wouldn't hold the car seats. And after all, we had less than a mile to drive to the edge of the National Forest.

Lucy sat on Mom's lap and Freddie sat on mine.

And on Freddie's lap, of course, was Buddy Wabbit. Mom says sometimes this stuffed bunny was like having a fourth kid because he had to go everywhere with us. Freddie danced him around, making his ears flop.

"Happy, happy, happy, happy!"

"Knock it off, Freddie," I said. "There's not enough room in here."

"Laissez les bons temps rouler!" Freddie shouted in Buddy Wabbit's horrible nasal voice. He'd picked up this line from Dad's Zydeco and Cajun records. It means "Let the good times roll!"

"Bill," Mom said, "he has an amazingly good French accent for a three-year-old."

"Not to mention his being a bunny," Dad added.

"Laissez les bons temps—"

"Dad, will you make him pipe down?"

Out of the corner of his mouth, Dad started singing. "Rabbit stew, rabbit stew . . . that's what I'd like to do with you . . ."

I laughed. That bunny voice drove us all nuts.

Buddy Wabbit kissed me. I batted him away.

"Grant us wisdom," Mom sang cheerfully, "grant us courage . . . for . . . the living of this hour. . . ."

"Freddie," Dad said, "I'm going to chain that rodent to your bedpost if you can't make him behave."

Freddie grinned like he didn't take this too seriously, but Buddy did seem to get a grip on himself after that.

Well, whether you buy your Christmas tree at a parking lot or go out in the woods and cut it yourself, the biggest part of the job is the same—the choosing. It's fun, though, and we were all feeling good as we tromped the spongy earth of the wet, fresh-washed forest.

Finally we settled on a huge Douglas fir. Well, not huge like they get if you leave them alone to grow for a few hundred years, but huge for something you're wrestling into the back of a pickup.

Dad liked to get the tallest tree we could fit inside our house, and since we live in a remodeled dairy barn with a two-story main room, that's pretty big! This one had a nice shape plus it was close to another good-size tree. We liked knowing that thinning it would actually help the other one grow bigger.

While Mom braced the trunk, Dad disappeared into the bottom branches to saw and mutter. Then, one at a time, he called each kid in for a turn at it. I always loved this part—breathing in the smell of the sap, getting my face sprinkled with cold raindrops from the shaking branches.

"Okay," Dad finally called from inside the branches, "everybody stand back now."

The tree cracked free as Mom and Dad eased it over. Dusk was falling as they were shoving the trunk end into the pickup bed, leaving the tip bouncing off the tailgate.

Mom brushed fir needles from her parka. "Don't we need to tie it?"

"It'll be okay," Dad told her. "It's such a short way."

"But Dad," I said, "what if it falls out?"

He slid the saw in beside the tree. "Then we stop and—

"Aaaaaaaahhhhh!" From somewhere above us, an eerie wail.

We stopped, frozen. Our faces turned up. Our eyes scanned the treetops.

Big Foot? That was my first thought. The huge and hairy creature that people say roams these forests. Or maybe an owl?

"Leeeet. . . . me. . . . hiiiiiide. . . ."

But those sounded like words.

Round-eyed, Lucy and Freddie looked at me. I looked at Mom and then Dad. They looked at each other over the hood of the truck.

Was this something to be scared of? I waited for them to laugh it off.

But they didn't.

For the first time that afternoon we were quiet enough to actually hear the wind in the high branches. It's a sound like far-off rushing rivers, a sad sound, like the earth sighing.

We listened, and the voice rose again, startling me even though I'd braced for it.

"Is that somebody singing or what?" I whispered a little desperately.

Nobody answered.

"Alfie?" Mom asked Dad.

He listened. "Must be."

Alfie. I'd heard about him. A guy who lived up on an old homestead near here and didn't come down much. Kids at school whispered strange stories about him.

"Okay, everybody," Dad said softly. "Let's go."

We packed into the truck cab, this time not minding the closeness. Our warm breath fogged the windows as we headed down the gravel road.

"Dad?" I said. "Why was he yelling like that? Or singing or whatever?"

"Well . . ." Dad drew it way out. "They say that's his way of talking to God, Robby. Every once in a while he likes to get up on his roof and say what's on his mind."

Lucy squawked. "Talk to God in the sky? Like, 'Yo! God!'"

"Lucy!" Mom smiled and frowned at the same time.

We were quiet the rest of the short ride home. All you could hear was the engine and the rustle against the back of the cab that let us know we hadn't lost the tree anywhere along the way.

It wasn't until later that evening, when the tree was up and the little guys were putting together a stuffed animal crèche and arguing over who should be Jesus, that Freddie realized the awful truth.

Buddy Wabbit was missing.

We searched the house and the truck. Nobody could recall seeing him after we got home.

Freddie stood at the window and peered into the dark.

"Lost in the woods," he said, and as we looked out

together, I wondered if he was thinking the same things I was: how big the forest was and how dark. I was thinking of that spooky voice, moaning into the starry night sky.

⸬ 4 ⸬

A Forbidden Subject

My teacher this year was new at Nekomah Creek, so none of us had known what to expect when we walked into that first day of fifth grade.

We found out fast! It was *Fasten your seat belts because we are taking off!*

Everything about Ms. Carlotti seemed electrified, from her wild, frizzy hair to the speedy, breathless way she talked. She hardly ever sat down, but spent the whole day pacing the room, flinging her arms and trailing scarves, as if her job of teaching and our job of learning were the most important, most exciting things in the world.

We were starting a unit on environmental problems now, and, to begin with, we were supposed to list out loud the ones we'd heard about. Ms. Carlotti made it plain she expected us to stretch our brains and come up with more than "roadside litter" and kindergarten stuff like that.

Now, some people might imagine Oregon as this nice, clean place with none of these problems, but that's not true at all. For one thing, we have a lot of fighting going on about whether we ought to save the forests or go ahead and cut them down for lumber.

The minute West Feikart said, "Overcutting of the forests," Darrel Miskowiec stuck up his hand.

"My dad says that's not a problem at all," he protested. "Trees are renewable. We're planting more all the time."

"Not fast enough," West shot back.

"Yes, sir!" Darrel's parents both work planting trees, see. To them trees are a crop to harvest, not something to get mushy about.

"And anyway, no matter how many trees you plant," West said, "tree farms aren't the same as old-growth forests. They don't have all the different kinds of plants and animals."

"Bio-diversity," I said without thinking. I'd heard that on a National Geographic TV show.

"Eeuuw!" Orin Downard mocked me. "Big words." He's this kid who lives in the next house down the road from us. For some reason, I'm the person he most enjoys picking on.

"And your idea of an environmental problem?" Ms. Carlotti prompted him.

"The problem," Orin said, "is people who want to save every dumb slimy slug and they don't give a darn whether people have jobs or not. My family's been loggers for three generations. What are we supposed to do if you won't let us cut trees?"

"Right," Darrel said, turning on me. "Anyway, you

like books so much. Where do you think paper comes from?"

I sank in my chair. "All I said was 'bio-diversity.' "

"Yeah, you don't have to put him down," Jesse Glenn said, "just because he knows the right scientific term."

I shot Jesse a grateful glance. It's a good feeling to have somebody like him stick up for you.

"Anyway," Jesse went on, "my dad says that at the rate the forests are being cut, there aren't going to be any jobs left in a few years anyway."

People got quiet. Everybody knew Jesse's dad was a scientist, and that was a sobering idea—no jobs in the woods. What if he was right?

Jesse's whole family was smart, in fact. His mom wrote articles for scientific magazines, and his brother went to Dartmouth College. Sitting there discussing ocean pollution, Jesse came across as somebody who ought to be taken seriously too.

Ocean pollution led in to Willow Daley talking about pollution of the rivers, then Ms. Carlotti said, "All right now, let's hear from some of you who haven't spoken. Krishnasamy?"

Krish is from India and his family recently bought the motel down at Fern Creek. When he just smiled, Ms. Carlotti didn't push him. Maybe he needed more time to get used to it here.

"Ben? What other problems? What about agriculture? Dairy farming?"

Ben's family had acres of green pastures full of black and white cows.

"Well," he said, "my dad says some scientists are complaining the atmosphere is getting wrecked because of cows belching and—uh—well, I better not say the word."

"Are we speaking, perhaps," Ms. Carlotti said, "of bovine flatulence?"

Everybody started laughing as she put it on the blackboard.

Ben's face got red. "My dad says it's not true, though. He says that's . . . that's . . ."

"A load of cow manure?" Jesse offered.

A hoot from Ms. Carlotti. Points for Jesse. I mean, lots of kids can make the class laugh. But to get the teacher to laugh, stay out of trouble yourself, and not have people hating you for being a teacher's pet— now that's a real trick.

"All right, then," Ms. Carlotti said, recovering herself, "let's do this." She put a question mark after "bovine emissions" on the list. "Maybe that could be your research project, Ben." She turned to the rest of the class. "Because you realize that's what we're leading to, a report from each of you. Now. Breanna. We haven't heard from you yet. What are your thoughts on all this?"

"Well . . ." Breanna glanced around. "In my church—"

"Speak right up, Breanna."

"In my church," Breanna said a little louder, "the minister tells us these problems are just signs. That's what the Bible says." Her voice was still on the soft side but confident. "Like what Willow was saying about the rivers getting polluted? It's right there in the Book of Revelations—*The rivers will become like the blood of a dead man.*"

Whoa. That shut everyone up. Even Ms. Carlotti.

I stared at Breanna. I'd always just thought of her as this quiet girl who had won every single spelling bee since first grade. I never knew she was thinking about things like *this*.

"So you see," she went on, "it's really no use arguing because it's just part of God's plan, and pretty soon the world's going to end anyway."

Dead silence. Then a couple of kids snickered, a nervous sound.

"Students," Ms. Carlotti warned them. "Let's respect the viewpoints of others." She cleared her throat. "I'm afraid, though, that on the subject of religion, the school board doesn't encourage us to—"

"And in the meantime," Lindsey said, "multiply and subdue the earth." She's Breanna's best friend. "We're the bosses of all the animals and birds and fish. That's what it says."

"What *what* says?" Ms. Carlotti asked, forgetting, I guess, about the school board.

"Well, the *Bible*," Lindsey said, as if this ought to be obvious.

"Forgive me," Ms. Carlotti said. "You might have been quoting from the Koran, you know. Or the Torah."

"The what?"

"Teddy? Can you tell us about the Torah?"

Teddy Singer cleared his throat. "It's, like, all the holy writings for the Jewish people."

"And the Koran," Jesse added, "is the sacred book of the Moslems."

"Very good!" Ms. Carlotti said, surprised and pleased. "Yes, we do have to realize there are many different religions in the world."

Lindsey crossed her arms over her chest. "Not in Nekomah Creek."

"At the Unitarian Church," Willow said, "we think being in charge of all the plants and animals means taking care of them."

"Well, *Unitarians*," Monica Sturdivant scoffed. "My dad says that's no church at all."

"It is to me!" Willow said.

Now, I don't usually sit around thinking *I'm a Presbyterian,* but all this choosing sides got me trying to remember what I'd heard at *our* church. For the Earth Day sermon last spring, the minister quoted from the Bible about God making the world and everything in it and deciding it was good. It was *all* good, the minister pointed out. Nothing in there about how we ought to get busy improving it by wiping out half the different kinds of plants and animals . . .

Orin and a couple of his buddies were still stuck on the fascinating subject of cow flatulence when the bell rang for lunch, and they burst into the hall with a lot of loud and realistic noises, making everyone cringe to the side as they charged through.

The rest of us seemed to drift around Breanna and Lindsey, not crowding, but making sure we were close enough to hear if they dropped any more end-of-the-world bombshells.

At the long lunch table where our class sat, it was as if we were all waiting.

Finally, I had to ask. "Do you really believe that stuff you said, Breanna?"

Her eyebrows went up behind her straight-cut bangs. "Of course I do."

Willow sniffed. "You're awful calm for somebody who's expecting the end of the world."

Breanna and Lindsey traded a quick, smiling glance.

"The thing is," Breanna said, "we know we're going to be saved."

We watched her, waiting for more.

"When the end comes," she said, "the people who go to our church and believe what we believe will just rise up and go to heaven with the Lord."

"That's right," Lindsey said. By now I was catching on she must go to that same church.

"So what happens to everybody else?" I said.

Breanna gave me a pitying look. "Haven't you heard of the everlasting lake of fire?"

"Uh, no."

"That's in hell, you know, where all the sinners will burn."

I looked down toward Jesse at the other end of the table, wondering what he was thinking of this. He didn't even seem to be listening. Probably just hurrying through lunch to beat it out to the soccer field.

"The sinners," Breanna went on, "and, you know, the people who don't come to our church and get right with God."

"They have to come to your particular church?" I asked. "No other?"

She sighed, getting impatient. "No, not just that one. We have churches all over the country, so they could go to one of those."

"What if they're Jewish?" my friend Rose Windom piped up. "Or Hindu or Buddhist?"

"Yeah," I said, wishing I'd thought of that. "Or Moslem?"

Breanna gave us a long, sad look, as if we were already goners. "I didn't make the rules," she said. "Don't blame me."

·:5:·

Change of Heart

Outside, I hunched my shoulders against the cold. Misty clouds drifted through the fir-covered ridges, and I noticed the dampness beading in Rose's long black hair.

"Boy," I said as we crossed the playground, "that was pretty weird, huh?"

"Yeah."

"You don't believe that stuff, do you?"

She looked insulted. "No!"

"Breanna sounded so sure, though."

"Her sounding sure doesn't make it true."

Good point. I couldn't help wondering, though, what it'd feel like to be so . . . *confident* about things. I wondered what the other kids thought. But church stuff was kind of personal. You'd feel funny running around quizzing people on the subject.

"So what are you going to do your environmental report on?" Rose asked.

I thought a moment. "Well, maybe something about how the streams get wrecked when they log right down to the water." I'd latched on to this topic mostly because of the idea I had for a great clay demonstration model. "What about you?"

"I think I'll report on how we can keep the dumps from filling up if we recycle more stuff. My mom's very big on that."

"Mine, too."

"It's like a game to her—seeing how long we can go before we have to break down and take a sack of garbage to the dump."

"Well, if keeping the dump from filling is your goal," I said, "my dad's the one who's really doing *his* part. He usually comes home from the landfill with more stuff than he started out with!"

Rose laughed. She really likes my dad. "And what about the play?" she said. "Are you trying out?"

"No way."

"But it's going to be fun. Especially with Ms. Carlotti as the director."

True, Ms. Carlotti could make just about *anything* fun. She was one of those teachers my parents talk about, the kind you'll probably remember all your life. Still . . .

"Drama isn't my thing," I said. "My mom's been bugging me about it for weeks, and Ms. Carlotti's been asking me too, but I just don't want to."

"Are you sure?" Rose said. "Oh, I wish you'd change your mind."

"Sorry."

Out on the soccer field, I could see Jesse kicking the ball around, warming up. He was easy to spot with his coppery hair. No one else had hair that color. Look at him, I thought. He never seemed to worry about anything—not his project, not the play, and certainly not any old lake of fire.

"Rose?" I said. "Do you guys go to church?" I couldn't remember her ever talking about it.

"No, but not because we're not religious. My mom says most of the regular churches don't feel right to her. See, we sort of think of God as female. You know, like God our Mother instead of God our Father."

"Oh. I guess I always thought of God as being like a man."

"Well, of course you would, if you always went to a church where they say *He* created the world and all that. But who knows? And Mom says it's easier for her to think of God being like a mother because mothers take care of you and she thinks of fathers as just bossing you around or leaving you."

"But my father takes care of me."

"I know, but my father left us. And my mother's father left her and *her* mom. So you can see why we'd feel that way."

I nodded, watching Jesse run across the wet grass of the soccer field. It's a funny thing about him. Most new kids act kind of shy, but Jesse had just come, looked around, and taken charge. He was always getting up a game or accidentally starting a fad by coming up with something new and cool. He was the first kid to have little plastic hand warmers for his pockets, for instance. The kind with a mysterious liquid that gets hot when you press a button? Now half the kids in school had them, and the other half had them on their Christmas wish lists.

I thought a lot about Jesse and why it was like this. Maybe part of his specialness came from everyone knowing he'd only be here a short time. His dad was doing an oceanographic research project. After this year, they'd go back to Massachusetts.

Another thing was that although he was smart and liked books as much as I did, nobody ever called him a bookworm. Probably because he was a terrific athlete too. I might have been jealous except that the very first time he came out and started lining up a game, *I* was the first person he chose for his team. That had never happened to me before in my whole life!

Rose didn't like Jesse as much as I did. "He's so bossy," she was always saying under her breath. But she probably would have liked him better if he was choosing *her*.

"Hey, Robbo!" he called now. "You're on my team!"

I fought off a grin as I trotted out to the field.

It was a good game. We all got wet to the knees and played hard enough to get winded. I even kicked a goal, thanks to Jesse. He could have kicked it in himself, but he passed the ball to me instead.

When the bell rang, we trooped back to the school, everybody red-cheeked and panting. Rose, who'd had to be on Darrel's team, walked on one side of me, and Jesse ran up on the other.

"So, Robbo," he said. "Trying out for the play this afternoon?"

"Nah. Don't think so."

"Aw, come on!" He tossed the soccer ball and practiced a header. "I'm going to."

I glanced at Rose, who pretended she wasn't listening.

"Well," I said. "Maybe I will."

"Hey, okay!" He punched my shoulder.

I didn't look at Rose after that.

·: 6 :·

A Mistake

So that's how I found myself between Rose and Jesse again that afternoon, this time on the stage.

Well, I was thinking, at least my mother will be happy.

Looking over the script, I'd decided *The True Spirit of Christmas* should have been called *The Theater Vaccine,* because this turkey was the perfect play to make sure a bunch of kids stayed away from theater for the rest of their lives. Why do writers insult kids' intelligence with this stuff? Where do they get the idea we're all dying to dress up as twerpy elves? Or go lurching around like a bunch of mechanical toys?

When we were finished reading the different parts for Ms. Carlotti, Monica Sturdivant led a new group up onto the stage.

Rose sank back into her chair. "She wants the same part I do—the Dancing Princess Doll." She sighed wistfully. "The script says the Princess Doll gets to dance in a spotlight all by herself."

A little later, as Ms. Carlotti explained the special dancing tryouts for this part, you could tell by the way the girls all leaned forward that the Princess Doll was what every single one of them wanted to be.

"Can you dance?" I whispered, eyeing Rose's hiking boots doubtfully. Even with her long, flowered skirts she never wears the sort of slipper shoes that make you picture twinkle-toeing around a stage.

"Good question," she said, as if she'd never really thought about it. "I guess we'll find out pretty soon, won't we?"

I took a deep breath. I wanted Rose to get the part, but I knew Monica had been taking dancing lessons since the day she stopped crawling and stood up. Last year at a school basketball game halftime she wore a black leotard and did a jazz routine to some loud, pounding music. And at the Tillamook County Fair she sang western songs in a cowgirl outfit. My mom says she's a born performer.

Still, when I watched Rose twirl around the stage in her socks, I thought her dancing was good enough. And she'd make a pretty Dancing Princess Doll, too, with her dark hair and rosy cheeks. Not that I could ever in a million years *tell* her that! When she came down and dropped into her seat beside me, I just leaned over and mumbled, "Good job."

Whoa. She blushed like I'd asked her to marry me or something!

I'll tell you, though, the light faded right out of her pop-bottle green eyes the minute Monica walked out onto the stage.

"Toe shoes," Rose breathed with a mixture of dismay and admiration. "Monica's dancing in toe shoes. Oh, I've always wished I could do that . . ."

At home that night I told Mom tryouts had gone okay, but the play itself was a joke. I could see by the faces she made as she read the script that she agreed, but still she couldn't hide how tickled she was I'd tried out.

"I'm sure this'll be better," she said, "when you kids bring it to life."

"Don't hold your breath."

Dad crawled out of the cardboard fort now occupying the main room. It was made from the boxes his new file cabinets had come in, the ones he'd bought to help sort tax papers. So far the cabinets were sitting in the guest room, empty, and Mom had taken to wondering out loud a lot whether the IRS man was really going to be all that impressed with a fort.

"Why did Ms. Carlotti choose this particular play?" Dad asked. "I'd've thought she'd be the type to come up with something better."

"Oh, the committee chose it and ordered the scripts before she was even hired this fall," Mom said. "I heard they had quite a time finding a play that wouldn't offend anyone."

"Yeah?" I said. "Well, this one offends *me*. It offends me by being so bad."

"Of course, it had to be something that steered clear of any religious themes," Mom said.

"They might even get in trouble doing Santa Claus and Christmas trees," Dad added.

"But everybody around here does Christmas," I said.

"I doubt the Singers do," Dad said. "Aren't they Jewish?"

"I guess. Ms. Carlotti asked Teddy something about the Torah today."

"We can't just automatically assume everybody celebrates Christmas," Dad pointed out.

"Or that they're Christian, the way we did when we were in school," Mom said. "Now, when I think about it, it amazes me how our school choir sang all sorts of religious songs and we never thought anything about it. But then, there weren't nearly the number of different religions represented in the schools. I remember when I was really little, somebody whispering about a girl being Catholic, for heaven's sake, like that was terribly strange and different."

"Oh, sure," Dad said. "Don't you remember what a stir it caused when John Kennedy ran for President? A Catholic?"

"Really?" I said. "I thought John Kennedy was everybody's hero."

Mom shook her head. "Not in the beginning."

"Well, anyway," I said, "I wasn't trying to get into some big discussion about church. I just wanted to say that I think *The True Spirit of Christmas* stinks!"

"I heard the committee had another play picked out," Mom said, "but then Jane Holter got upset because it had a witch in it."

"You mean Breanna's mom?"

"Yes."

Lucy's blond head popped up from a hatch in the fort. "Breanna's mom's a witch?"

Mom laughed. "No, no, Honey . . ."

"But what's wrong with witches?" I said. "Was it too much like a Halloween play?"

"Oh, no. Jane Holter won't stand for witches *any* time of year. She has a whole list of things that are against her religion—witches, druids, magic . . ."

"What's wrong with magic?" I said. "It's just pretend."

"Oh, I know that, Robby. But she probably has some Bible verse about it. Some people just feel safer keeping to strict rules from the Bible."

I frowned, thinking. "But don't *we* believe in the rules of the Bible?"

"Well, yes, the basic, underlying ones. But some of the rules in the Bible have to do with life as it was lived two thousand years ago. And the way I see it, God gave us the brains to sort out which is which. For instance, when I was your age and going to the Episcopal church, all the women and girls had to wear hats to services, because in the Bible only bad women went around with their heads uncovered."

"That's sort of silly."

"But it was a rule, so people were afraid to break it. Your grandmother used to get so annoyed. She said it made church one big hat contest. Well, finally they gave it up."

"No more hats?"

"Only if you want to wear one, I guess. And I haven't heard any reports of large numbers of hatless women being struck by lightning bolts during services, either! So you see, it doesn't hurt to *think* about rules and whether we ought to change them."

All this had given me plenty to brood about, and later that night, when Mom was busy with the little guys, I found Dad alone in the kitchen, checking his recipes, writing up a grocery list.

"Dad," I said. "Do you believe in hell?"

"Hell? You mean like a fiery place run by a guy in a red suit and a pitchfork?"

"Well, yeah. Like where you go if you're bad. You know, when you die."

He scrunched up his face. "Nah."

"Breanna Holter does. You know the one you were

talking about her mom? She says anybody who doesn't believe like she does is going to hell."

"Oh, for Pete's sake."

"She said that right in the cafeteria today."

"Well, if she's right, hell's going to be awfully crowded, isn't it? Because I'll tell you, Robby, the world's full of a lot of good people who don't necessarily agree with the Holters."

He pawed through the bread drawer, scribbled on his list.

"Don't you think that's kind of mean?" I said. "Going around *Nyeah, nyeah, I'm going to heaven and you're not?*"

"It isn't *my* idea of being charitable, but I guess she has a right to think what she wants."

"Huh. And say it, too, I s'pose."

"That's the way it works. Even if we don't like hearing it, it's safest to make sure everybody gets to say what they think."

"Well," I said. "I'm glad *you* don't believe in hell."

"Not in Breanna's sense, no." He looked out the kitchen window into the darkness. "Oh, no, I'm afraid we humans are quite capable of making our own hells right here on earth."

"You mean like wars and stuff?" I'd heard that saying: War is hell.

"That's right. War and all the other lousy stuff you hear on the news. People hurting other people, hurting themselves . . ."

He sounded so sad. I felt bad I'd brought it up.

"And then there's the hell people mean when they say 'I went through hell.' That's real enough." He turned around and leaned against the corner of the counter, arms crossed over his chest. "Hell for me would be if . . . well, if I ever lost you, Robby. Or your mother. Or Freddie and Lucy."

"Oh." Dad doesn't get serious like this very often. When he does, I feel sort of weird. Maybe that's why I'm not real quick with the heavy-duty questions.

Suddenly his voice got chipper. "So!" He squinted into the refrigerator. "Am I making any sense?"

"Sure." I shrugged. "I guess."

He opened the freezer. "Well, what do you know. Good old Tillamook ice cream. Isn't chocolate peanut butter your favorite?" He took off the lid. "Hmm. Looks like just enough for two generous servings."

"Yes!"

As he dished it up he said, "Your mom sure is tickled about you trying out for the play."

"Da-ad."

He stopped. "What?"

"No more depressing talk, okay?"

Well, I'm sorry to say I got a part. The next morning, there was my name—Robby Hummer—typed on the cast list opposite my name in the play—Elroy, the Head Elf.

All the other kids were jumping around, excited to see which part they'd be playing. Of course some, like Rose, were disappointed.

"Oh, well," she said. "The Rag Doll's a fun part too. And the costume will be easier for my mom to do. Sequins and sparkly princess things probably cost a lot."

The Dancing Princess Doll role had gone to

Monica, naturally, who looked pleased but not surprised.

"I prayed for it," we heard her say to Lindsey as they walked away. "Sure enough, the Lord came through."

Rose and I traded a look.

"Personally," I said out of the corner of my mouth, "I'm giving credit to the dancing lessons."

Rose sagged against the wall as I studied the cast list.

"I don't see Jesse's name," I said. "That's funny. He read better than anybody."

"Sh!" Rose said, straightening up. "Here he comes."

Jesse sauntered over and glanced at the list. "Hey, Robbo! Head Elf. Way to go."

I waited to see what he'd do when he saw he hadn't gotten a part.

"You guys are going to have fun," he said. "Wish I could be in it too."

"It must be a mistake, Jesse. Didn't Ms. Carlotti say everybody who wanted to be in the play would get to be *something*?"

"Yeah, that's right." Suddenly he caught on. "Oh, hey, it's not like you think. See, last night when I got home, my dad reminded me I've got these computer classes starting next week. We had to call Ms. Carlotti and tell her not to cast me."

My face flushed red hot. I didn't even know why. I felt Rose watching me but I wouldn't look at her.

"I wish you'd told me," I grumbled.

He blinked. "Why?"

"I don't know."

Rose had spread on a big, bright smile. "So, Robby," she said, "you think your mom can make you a good elf costume?"

A fresh wave of gloom washed over me. "I'm sure she can."

·· 7 ··

My Brilliant Idea

A TV beer commercial, of all things. That's what set Freddie off.

Maybe you've seen the ad—big, handsome horses pulling a sleigh through powdery snow? Every time those sleigh bells started jingling, my mom would get weepy. I kept wondering if she was still in a quick-to-cry mood because of dumb old Galaxy Greetings.

One night I was in the kitchen, stirring up a big batch of flour and salt paste for my healthy-streams project when it happened again—first the music and sleigh bells, then the sniffling. "Mom," I said, "how come you always cry over this commercial?"

"Oh, that song," Mom said, drifting into the kitchen. " 'I'll Be Home for Christmas.' It makes me realize how lucky we are we *will* be home for Christmas—I think you'll need more salt in that. Then I start worrying about all the people who won't, you know, because they don't *have* a home. And then I think about the Christmas your grandmother got out of the hospital on Christmas Eve . . .''

By now I had the picture, but my mom always has to keep explaining, going on about her good feelings and her sad feelings, squeaking off into tears again as she tested the consistency of my dough.

I had no idea Freddie was paying attention to any of this, but a couple of hours later, after he and Lucy had been put to bed, he came dragging back out, his face stricken.

''Freddie.'' Dad looked up from his pamphlet, *How to Survive a Tax Audit.* ''What's the matter, Honey?'' It wasn't like Freddie to get out of bed.

''Buddy,'' he cried. ''Buddy's lost!''

Mom and I looked at each other. He'd just now figured this out?

''Buddy won't be home for Christmas!'' He was crying so hard, the tears just sprang out. It was like it had finally hit him that Buddy was gone for good.

Well, it killed me. I felt so helpless, standing there with my hands dripping blobs of flour and salt paste. Mom and Dad and I told him Buddy might turn up yet. We pointed out that, after all, we *do* have lots of other stuffed animals. Dad tried to distract him with the funny cartoons in his pamphlet showing the tax auditor as a gorilla.

But Freddie wouldn't cheer up. He finally just wore down.

After Mom carried him back to bed, I said, ''Dad, we've got to do something.''

''Like what?''

''I don't know. Go look for the bunny or something.''

"Robby, don't you think I did? I spent two hours tromping those woods the morning after we got the tree."

"Oh."

"We were all over the place up there. If he set it on the truck bumper or something, it could have fallen off anywhere on the way home. So I walked that whole ditch."

All this reminded me of my old Bunky Bear, who got wet and rotten inside and had to be thrown away. Of course, that was ages ago and it doesn't bother me anymore. Even so, seven years later, I can still remember how bad my chest ached when Mom and Dad broke it to me he was gone. I felt like *I* was the one who was rotten inside.

That's probably the way Freddie was feeling now.

Lying in bed up in my loft that night, I wished that somehow the bunny would miraculously show up. I guess, at some point, the wishing slipped over into praying.

Now, to be honest, I don't pray much. I try to if we're in church and they say, okay, now let us pray, but still my mind wanders. I do remember praying in a real serious way one time when I overheard my folks talking about some little girl who had leukemia and might die. That was so awful and scary—a little kid dying. I prayed really hard she wouldn't. That was a long time ago, though. I don't know if my praying did any good, because I never had the nerve to ask. I guess even now I'm afraid of the answer.

But a lost bunny didn't seem important enough to bug God about. It didn't compare to all the things a million times worse happening all over the world every day. Still, it mattered a lot to Freddie. And wasn't it at least as important as asking to be chosen as the Dancing Princess Doll?

"So what's the deal about prayers?" I asked Dad the next day.

"The deal?"

"Yeah. I mean, it's not like they get answered every time, right? It's not like ordering a hamburger and fries." All you have to do is pray for something once without getting it to figure this out.

Dad kind of hemmed and hawed. Then he told me a story about a guy who was sitting on the roof of his house as flood waters rose around him. People kept offering to rescue him, but he'd always say, "No, thanks. I've prayed to the Lord and the Lord will save me." Finally he drowned, and at the pearly gates he complained to God. "I prayed and had faith in you, Lord. Why didn't you help me?" God said, "Hey, I sent you two boats and a helicopter. What more did you want?"

I laughed. Then I said, "But what does it mean?"

"Well, to me it means maybe we shouldn't worry about our prayers being answered. Maybe we ought to just try to do what we're supposed to be doing, taking care of each other. Because, who knows? A person might be the answer to somebody else's prayer without even knowing it."

Well, I *wanted* to help be Freddie's answer, but how?

It was the next afternoon that I got my brilliant idea. It was a no-rehearsal day for me, and I was talking to Dad while he sorted the laundry.

"Hey, Dad," I said, interrupting my own story

about Jesse's newest computer game. "I think you just put Lucy's shirt in Freddie's basket."

"Oh, well. I don't worry about keeping them straight when they have these matching ones."

"But Lucy's World Wildlife shirt has a stain on it."

Dad shrugged. "Freddie never seems to notice."

Right then that old light bulb flashed over my head. The kids were glued to their PBS shows so I sneaked into their room and found Lucy's nameless bunny wedged headfirst into the seat of a fire engine. I had picked out the two stuffed animals for the twins on the day they were born, and they had started out identical—the bunnies, not Freddie and Lucy—but somehow Lucy never got attached to hers. Not that it looked brand-new, because all the animals got thrown around, but it certainly didn't have that loved-to-a-frazzle look like Freddie's.

Well, I could fix that. If Freddie didn't know which shirt was which, maybe I could fool him about the bunnies too.

But how to make this one look loved? For starters, although it bothered me to do it, I pulled out his whiskers and the threads that made his mouth and nose. Then, with scissors, I ripped his side seam in just the spot where Freddie likes to poke his finger when he drifts off to sleep.

"Robby!" Dad said, catching me at it. "What on earth are you doing?" And when I explained my idea he said, "Well, I guess it *might* work."

I studied the bunny. So far, so good, but he still didn't look right. How could I duplicate all the hours of cuddling, all the spills and smearings Buddy Wabbit had survived?

This called for drastic measures.

I got a piece of twine and knotted it around the bunny's neck. "I'm going for a bike ride, Dad."

I tied the other end of the twine to my bike and pedaled down the drive to the plank bridge, the bunny bouncing along behind me.

At the road I stopped. If I went down Nekomah Creek Road toward the highway, I'd have to go by Orin Downard's house. I headed up for the school instead. A couple of loops around the playground and parking lot ought to do the trick!

It was turning out to be a nice day. For the moment, anyway, the sun was out. The air smelled fresh and clean and I was in a good mood. Yes sir, a boy and a bunny, out for a spin on a brisk winter's afternoon.

After I bumpbumpbumped through the covered bridge, I stopped to check the progress. Seemed like the bunny kept hitting one spot, so I retied him, this time around his cotton tail. I needed him more well done.

Hey, I was feeling great now, like a take-charge kind of guy. Dad was right. You couldn't just sit around wishing and praying for solutions, you had to get out and do something! At the school, I circled the gravel parking lot, empty except for a few teachers' cars.

I was just about to head home when who should come out of the front door of the school but my old fourth-grade teacher, Mrs. Perkins.

Uh-oh.

Actually, "uh-oh" is pretty much what pops into my head every time I see her. Because, unfortunately, she is nothing like Ms. Carlotti. That is to say, if I ever

tell stories about Mrs. Perkins in public when I am grown up, I will probably not be using her real name.

"Robert Hummer!" She put a fist on her hip. "For-e-ver-more!"

"Uh, hi, Mrs. Perkins." I slowed to a respectful stop.

"What are you doing with that poor bunny?"

"Oh, I'm just . . . uh, fixing him up for my little brother."

She looked at the dirty bunny, tied by his tail. She looked at me. "I suggest you untie that bunny and get along home."

I did like she told me and pedaled slowly away. She passed me in her car just before the covered bridge, but I kept my eyes on the road, breathing in her car's exhaust. Mrs. Perkins has never liked me. Oh, well, I thought, what do I care if she thinks I'm weird? Especially if it's for such a good cause.

Remembering that I was close to the moment of triumph, I stood on the pedals for speed.

At home, I raced in, pretending to be breathless and excited. "Freddie! Look who I found!"

Freddie came running, all lit up.

He sucked in his breath. "Buddy! Oh, Buddy Boy!"

He threw himself at me, grabbing the rabbit. He hugged it and danced.

I beamed, the happy hero.

Then Freddie stopped. He stared hard at the bunny. He looked up accusingly at me.

I tried to make my voice sound innocent. "What's the matter?"

"Dis not Buddy," he said, dropping it on the floor.

"Come on, Freddie, what makes you so sure?"

"Doesn't *smell* like Buddy."

Smell? For Pete's sake!

"Dat just Lucy's bunny, all beat up."

"He didn't buy it," I told Dad later out in his wood shop.

"Yeah? Well, we're talking true love here, you know. Probably no way to pack three years of it into one twenty-minute frenzy."

So that was the end of my brilliant idea—except that when Lucy caught on she had a fit.

"My bunny! My little poorest bunny!" As if this had always been her most favorite toy. When she finally stopped wailing, she glared at me. "I'm crying so hard," she said, "and now my eyeball is broken!"

·· 8 ··

Close Encounter

I stood on a chair by the sewing machine, modeling my fake-suede elf booties for my mother.

Lucy ran a little plastic car up my leg.

"Hey, don't," I said. "That tickles." The driver, I noticed, was not the usual peg person, but half a dill pickle. "Are you almost done, Mom? I need to work on my project."

My forest model was starting to take shape. Half of it would show a healthy stream, the other half a stream turned into a muddy ditch by badly planned logging. The hills and gullies I'd formed on Saturday night had now dried rock hard on the sheet of plywood and were ready for painting.

"I just can't seem to get these toes right," Mom said. "Lucy, Honey, could you drive that somewhere else, please?"

Mom was determined the bootie toes should curl

back and have dangling bells, but they kept flopping over.

"You don't have to knock your lights out, Mom," I said, sitting to tug the boots off. "Really."

"But Robby, you *are* the Head Elf."

"Don't remind me."

"Robby . . ." Dad eyed me over the top of the newspaper. We'd already had a little private talk about how making my costume had distracted Mom from her Galaxy Greetings gloom and how anything that cheered up one member of a family was bound to make things nicer for everyone else.

"I'm just thinking she'd probably rather be painting her pictures." I bugged my eyes out. "Okay?"

Nice try, Dad's look said. We both knew she'd been putting in long hours trying to finish as many paintings as possible for her special gallery showing.

"Oh, heavens, I can paint for the rest of my life," Mom said cheerfully, not picking up on any of this. "But how many chances will I get to make the world's most terrific elf suit?"

I gave Dad a sick smile.

"Maybe the stuffing isn't enough," Mom said. "Maybe we need a little wire in there . . ."

When Mom gets going on a costume, there's no stopping her. At Halloween, I always appreciate it. But this time . . .

She flipped through the costume books she'd brought home from the library. "I can't believe my luck in finding this terrific suede on sale . . ."

I shuffled to the art supply cupboard. "I wish I wasn't even in the play."

"Oh, now, Robby," Mom said. "You'll get out there under those lights and you'll love it."

"How do you know?" I sorted through the plastic containers of poster paint—green, brown, yellow, maybe some black to mix in. . . .

"Well, I'm just remembering how exciting it always was for me. The smell of the greasepaint, as they say. The roar of the crowd . . ."

"But, Mom! I'm not you!"

"He must take after me," Dad said, grabbing Freddie and bouncing him on his knee. "Did I ever tell you about the time they tried to make me play the piano for the school choir at an assembly? 'Cielito Lindo,' that was the song. It took a couple of weeks of heavy-duty goofing off during rehearsals, but finally I managed to get myself kicked out. Just in time too!"

"Bill, honestly! Don't tell him that story."

"*Ay, ay, ay, ay!*" Dad sang. "*Canta y no llores!* Don't you think that's a good one, Freddie? Spanish for 'sing and don't cry!' "

"Besides," Mom went on, "I think it's a shame that with all your musical talent, you never want to share it with anybody."

"Hey! Don't I practice my accordion every night for the kids while they're in the bathtub?" Freddie was crawling all over him now, wedging in behind the sofa cushions. "Freddie, for Pete's sake. What is it?"

"Looking for Buddy," Freddie said.

"But he's wost," Lucy said. " 'Member?"

Freddie stuck his chin out. "I know dat." Then, suddenly aware of his audience, he turned on a fakey, singsong cheer. "I think I go in my room." Bouncing from the sofa, he marched off.

"Mom," I said quietly, "I think he's going in there to cry."

Mom gave Dad one of those Concerned Looks. "I think so too."

Well, gee. If he'd whined around about the bunny I'd probably be saying *Oh, gimme a break.* But somehow those shiny brown eyes, trying so hard not to blink off the tears . . .

After the little guys were in bed and I had the base coat on my forest model, I took a black, felt-tipped pen and drew a lost bunny poster. I pointed out Buddy's identifying characteristics, like the fact that his embroidered mouth was history, for example. *Warning:* I wrote. *Blends in with dirt. Easily mistaken for something somebody threw away.* Also I drew a picture of Freddie looking pathetic.

I backed up and squinted. In spite of this being a sorry situation, I couldn't help admiring my work. I guess I am a pretty good artist. It's probably the one thing about me Jesse envies. He had a hard time in first grade, he says, because his teacher didn't even realize he was smart on account of his pictures and his handwriting being so sloppy. So he has always acted impressed with my artwork, and that makes me feel good.

Now, under the picture of Freddie, I put: *Sad kid loses lifetime buddy. REWARD!!!* I didn't know what the reward would be, but if somebody showed up with Buddy, I'd think of something.

I got my mom to run off copies at work the next day, then I rode up and down Nekomah Creek Road on my bicycle, putting the fliers in the newspaper boxes.

When Dad asked if I wanted to ride down to the post office with him to pick up a package, I hid one of the fliers under my jacket until we got in the truck.

"Whatcha got there?" Dad said.

"This," I said, pulling it out. "For the post office bulletin board. I didn't want Freddie to see it."

"Oh. Right."

We weren't talking about bunnies at all at our house these days. Mom had even hidden one of the kids' favorite books, *Home for a Bunny.*

"This poster's really our last hope," I said to Dad,

instinctively hunching down as we passed Orin's house. "I'm going to put up a couple at school too."

Dad kept his eyes on the twisty road. "You know, Robby, it isn't your fault he dropped his rabbit."

"I know. But doesn't it get to you, the way he was crying when he got out of bed the other night?"

"Well, sure."

"And I keep catching him with his finger in his mouth. He'd given that up, remember? Now he's back at it, always staring out at the woods, looking so sad."

"Yeah, well, he'll just have to get over it."

Maybe Dad was too old to remember how kids feel about stuff like this.

I stared straight ahead. "You called his bunny a rodent."

"What if I did? He's not *lost* because of that. And to be honest, I don't miss that awful voice one bit."

"I do," I lied. Now I felt bad, remembering how I'd laughed at Dad's rabbit stew jokes.

"Some things you can't fix," Dad said. "The bunny's lost and I'm afraid that's all there is to it."

I pressed my lips tight. Then I said, "Rabbits aren't rodents anyway."

At the post office, I did some rearranging on the bulletin board to make room for my poster. I'd cut a little fringe along the bottom with our phone number and address on each one.

Dad was standing in line at the window behind an old man who was picking up a huge pile of packages.

I sidled over to Dad to get a better look at the guy. He had a long braid and a beard, mostly gray, and deep crinkles around his eyes. He wore overalls and a blue work shirt with little flowers embroidered on the collar.

I gave Dad a questioning look. In return, he put on that blank, grown-up expression that means "We aren't going to talk about this now."

At one point the guy looked down, dark eyes boring right into me.

I flushed and glanced away.

It took him three trips to get his stuff out to his truck.

"Give you a hand?" Dad said after the first, but the man waved him off, passing close enough that I got a whiff of his damp, musty smell—rain and earth and maybe cigarettes. His quick step through the swinging door showed he wasn't as old as I'd first thought, although he did have a slight limp.

On his final trip he paused at the bulletin board. Holding his last packages to the side, he cranked his face forward on his neck, peering at the notices.

After he'd gone, the postmaster leaned his elbow on the counter and spoke in a low voice, as if the man might overhear from the parking lot. "Buys everything out of catalogs. Puts it all on credit cards so he won't have to shop in stores."

Dad looked down at me. "That was Alfie."

Whoa. The guy in the woods who wails from his rooftop? I shivered, staring out the glass door. I didn't know anyone who'd ever actually seen him, although kids told plenty of scary stories about him at school.

"Keeps to himself," the postmaster said as we watched the old pickup pull onto 101. "Only comes down every few months or so. 'Nam vet, I've heard. Just likes to sit up there and keep an eye on things with his binoculars." He plopped a big box on the counter. "Okay. Hummer. Nekomah Creek Road. Looks like this is the one you're after."

But I was hardly paying attention. I was thinking of old Alfie, up on his roof, singing his strange songs to God.

9

Mystery Call

I eyed the package nervously as Mom and Dad cut away the strapping tape. Looked like my aunt and uncle had mailed their gifts ahead to save lugging them on the plane.

Mom opened the top flaps. "Oh, no! Peanuts! These Styrofoam things make me crazy!"

Dad reached in for the first gift-wrapped box.

"Wait, Bill!"

Too late. The snowy white pellets were already cascading over the sides.

"Ya!" Lucy started throwing them.

Dad pulled out a second box.

Freddie grabbed a couple of fistfuls of Styrofoam and tossed them into the air. "It's snowing!"

Mom groaned. "You know how they stop us from driving into California with fresh fruit in the car? I think these peanuts ought to be turned back at the Oregon border."

"Okay, Robby, here's yours." Dad held out a package wrapped in red paper printed with green holly wreaths.

Reluctantly, I took it. Every year my California cousins send weird clothes—wild socks or suspenders or baggy balloon pants. Mom says that living in Marin County, they're on "the cutting edge" of fashion. Huh. Guess that puts me on the dull edge, with my plain old blue jeans. Only since Jesse came have I even switched from my standard striped polo shirts to T-shirts like most of the kids wear.

So sweating out thank-you notes for wild and crazy clothes has always been tough. The thought of having to thank my cousins in person panicked me.

"What's the matter?" Mom said.

"Well, they'll be watching when I open this and I'll have to say something nice."

"Yes," Mom said. "That's the usual procedure."

"But what if it's something totally outrageous?"

Mom shrugged. "Practice ahead of time saying 'Hey, this is neat. Thanks a lot.'"

"You want me to lie?"

"Uh, yes."

"Great."

"Now, Honey, we've talked about white lies . . ."

"And there's always the chance," Dad said, "it really *is* something neat."

"Dad. Why would this year be any different?"

"Give them a break, okay? They don't see you often enough to know what you like. For all we know, they hate what we send them."

I looked at the picture of our cousins on the piano, Cameron in jazzy clothes and Cassandra in a fluffy pink dress. Her curled blond hair was held in a band with a truly dumb-looking puff on it.

Maybe I *should* give them a break. It's probably not fair to call my cousins bad news. It's true I have some less than happy memories of them—Cassandra showing off for being able to read when I still couldn't. And Cameron, who's a year younger, chasing me with his popper gun the whole time we visited. But I hadn't seen them since before the twins were born, so I really didn't know what they were like by now. I didn't remember them looking like this picture, anyway. In my mind, Cassandra was a long-legged girl in jeans who could make it hand over hand from one end of the monkey bars to the other while I was still having to drop off in the middle.

Dad stuffed the box of peanuts into a closet, then turned back to the rest of us. "Well, this has certainly been an exciting day for me."

We waited. Obviously, there was more to this.

"My ants came!"

"Yay!" The twins jumped up and started dancing around.

"Daddy, where are they?" Lucy said.

"In the fridge, chilling out. The directions said that would make them sleepy so you can transfer them into the ant farm without them escaping all over the place."

"Bill!" Mom said. "We were going to work on the taxes tonight."

"Well, that was before the ants came, wasn't it?"

"Let's get 'em," Freddie said.

Mom glowered, scraping up stray peanuts. "Help me with these stupid things, will you, Robby?"

While Dad and the twins went off to set up the ant farm, the two of us raked Styrofoam.

"Ouch!" we heard Dad saying upstairs. "These little suckers bite!"

"Too bad," Mom muttered sarcastically.

When the phone rang, I jumped up.

"Oh, boo hoo!" a voice squeaked over the wires. "I'm a little lost bunny and I can't find my way home!"

I pulled the receiver away from my ear and stared at it. I could just see Orin Downard's ugly mug. But how did he know about the bunny? Because I certainly did not put a flyer in *his* box!

"Oh, boo hoo hoo!"

"Very funny!"

Mom looked up. "Robby, what on earth?"

I made a face, listening to the muffled snorts of laughter over the line.

"Oh, heeelp! I'm vewy, vewy scared!"

"Orin, you oughta—you oughta—" And then, because I can never think of the right thing to say fast enough, I just hung up.

·:10:·

Something to Hide

"Do the play!" Lucy demanded at breakfast. "Tell the dumb parts!"

"Okay, you guys would love this." I took my plate to the counter. "Yesterday the kids who play Santa's toys practiced their song and dance number. They skip around like this and run down the stage steps." I demonstrated, leading them out to the main room. "They sing, 'For joy! For joy! It's great to be a toy! I'll soon be riding in Santa's sleigh, to a little girl or boy!' "

Freddie laughed. "Again!"

So I did it a bunch more times, skipping around the Christmas tree.

"For joy! For joy!" Freddie and Lucy flung out their arms and whirled in a tippy-toe dance that reminded me of Snoopy the dog dancing for his supper in "Peanuts."

Lucy posed on the back of the sofa. "For joy!"

Freddie slid down the banister. "For joy!"

Mom came out from the kitchen. "For Pete's sake! Robby, you need to get going for school."

"But watch now, Mom. They can already do the whole thing. Go ahead, guys."

And then they wouldn't do it! Kids.

Monica's mother was in charge of costumes, and when she showed up at play practice after school that day, it sounded like she and Ms. Carlotti were arguing. No heavy-duty yelling or anything, but I heard a lot of that fakey polite talk grown-ups use when they disagree.

Also Ms. Carlotti was having trouble with two or three of the third-grade bonbons, so I guess I didn't pick a very good time to start in again, telling her how I thought we ought to rewrite quite a bit of the play.

"It's just so dated," I told her. "Did you notice that this was written way back in the forties?"

"Yes, Robby," she said, fluttering her eyes shut like the lights were bothering her. "I believe you've already brought your concerns on this matter to my attention several times."

"Just trying to be helpful."

A small sigh escaped her. "The most helpful thing you could do would be to simply learn your own part and let us worry about the rest."

Ouch. Ever notice how one sharp look from someone you like can hurt worse than all kinds of grief from a person you don't care about at all?

∴

Backstage, while we were standing around waiting for our turns to go on, a bunch of us started discussing Christmas trees.

"Ours is about fifteen feet tall," I bragged, glad for something to help me forget about Ms. Carlotti being annoyed with me. "My dad put in special permanent hooks on the walls and ceiling to anchor it."

"Wow," Rose said. "I didn't know you could buy them that big."

"You probably can't." I couldn't help squaring my shoulders. "We cut it ourselves."

"Yeah?" Ben said. "Where?"

"Up off Homestead Road."

Monica's head whirled around. "You went up *there*?"

"Well, yeah," I said, startled by her shocked expression. "It *is* National Forest past that orange gate. And we had a permit."

"I don't mean *that*." She went up on her toe shoes, then down. Up. And down. "I mean, I'd never go *near* the place. That's where that old hippie pervert lives."

"What are you talking about?"

"Old Alfie. Haven't you heard of him?"

"Well, yeah," I said, conscious of everyone following our little debate, "but who says he's a pervert?"

"Come on," Monica said. "He lives all alone? He does sewing stuff?"

"So what?" Funny how I suddenly felt called to defend the guy. "He's not hurting anybody."

"Oh, yeah? My brother knows a kid who went for a hike up there and never came back."

"Who?" I demanded. "What was his name?"

"Well, I don't remember now, but it's true."

"Can you prove it?"

"Robby! Are you calling my brother a liar? Besides . . ." She stopped her fancy footwork, glanced around, and lowered her voice like she was letting us in on a big mysterious secret. "We also know these people who picked Alfie up hitchhiking one time. When they stopped to let him out, he'd disappeared. Into thin air!"

Everyone stared at her.

"I don't believe that," I said, but my voice sounded small.

"Well, Robby, everybody knows he stands up on his roof yelling like a crazy man."

"Yeah? So? He's praying, for your information."

This stopped her, but only for a moment. "Funny way to pray," she muttered, and then added, "No, he's hiding something for sure."

"You don't know that." I was looking down at those dancing shoes of hers Rose admired so much. Up close they were really kind of grimy. "Anyway, you shouldn't say bad things about somebody you don't even know."

"Oh, and I suppose you *do* know him."

"No, not really." I stuck my hands in my back pockets. "I did see him at the post office yesterday, though."

Silence.

"You *did*?" Willow said. "Hey, what's he look like?"

So then I had everyone's attention. Monica had plenty of juicy stories, sure, but I was the one who had actually seen the notorious Alfie.

∴

When I got home from school, I went out to find Dad in his wood shop, where the air had a good, sawdusty smell.

"Dad," I said, "is Alfie a pervert?"

"*What?*"

"Monica says he's a weirdo and he must be hiding something."

"I don't think anybody knows much about Alfie." He blew the dust off the wood frame he'd just sanded. "I sure wouldn't count on Monica being the authority." After I repeated her stories, he said, "Oh, Robby, if a kid disappeared around here, don't you think we'd know about it? And that hitchhiker story is as old as the hills."

"It is?"

"Yes, and the thing is, you'll never hear it from the person who was actually there. It's always something that happened to somebody else."

"It does make an interesting story," I said.

"Of course! That's why people keep telling it. But as for Alfie, I think the poor guy just wants to be left alone. He probably likes the quiet up there after what he's been through. The war, I mean."

Sometimes people say "the war" like you're supposed to know which one. But there've been so many! And at our house we quit keeping track of them on TV after the time Freddie asked when the big tanks were going to come up Nekomah Creek Road.

"Didn't the postmaster say he was a 'Nam vet?" I asked. "Like Vietnam? That war was a long time ago, wasn't it?"

"Not to some people," Dad said. "Some folks still

have that war right there with them like a bad dream."

"And that makes them want to be alone?"

"Could. Now *I* wouldn't want to live alone, but—"

"Honey?" It was Mom, sticking her head in. "Oh, hi, Robby. I didn't even know you were home. Bill, could you help the twins with the ants? I really need to keep painting."

"Sure, sure."

Dad and I went inside.

"What was I saying?" Dad asked. "Oh, how I wouldn't want to live alone—"

"Daddy!" Freddie hollered from upstairs. "Lucy's giving them too much food!"

"But live and let live, I say, and if that's the way Alfie wants it—"

"Daddy! Quick!"

"Actually," Dad said to himself, climbing the stairs, "a day or two alone might be fun to try sometime. . . ."

·11·

Pointy Ears

"Rag Doll!" Ms. Carlotti called from the darkness of the auditorium, and Rose walked out onto the stage. Ms. Carlotti and Mrs. Sturdivant were conducting this little parade to see how each kid's costume looked under the lights.

What a way to spend a Saturday morning, I was thinking, standing in the wings with the others, my nose wrinkled against the stink of that greasepaint makeup Mom's always raving over.

"Rose, you look darling," Ms. Carlotti said.

Exiting toward us, Rose did a floppy-legged dance shuffle, leading with the palms of her mitteny doll hands.

"Your mom must've worked hours and hours on that," Willow said, fingering a fold of Rose's patchwork skirt.

Rose nodded happily, the stitches of her doll

makeup curving at the corners of her mouth. "Now I'm glad I'm the Rag Doll."

Orin Downard's little sister Peggy, a snowflake, had an especially good costume, too, thanks to their mom being a dressmaker.

Ben was supposed to be one of those old-fashioned toy soldiers. His costume looked like his mom spent about twenty minutes on it, but he didn't seem to care. I kind of admired his attitude.

And then there was Monica. Her costume reminded me of that dress worn by the good witch in the "Wizard of Oz" movie—white and poofy and it stuck out about a mile around her. People could hardly help bumping into her backstage and every time they did, she'd mutter, "Well, excuuuuse you."

"Elroy, the Head Elf," Ms. Carlotti called.

I felt naked in my green tights. The makeup moms had reddened my nose and attached bits of putty to my ears to make them pointy. Nobody had warned me about that! I trudged out to the masking-tape X and stood there staring down at my perfectly curled-back elfie toes.

"Yo! Robby the Christmas Elf!"

My head snapped up. I squinted into the darkness at the back of the auditorium. I'd know that voice anywhere. Orin Downard. My pointy ears burned.

"All right now," Ms. Carlotti said mildly, turning toward Orin. "If we're not part of this production, let's run along. Robby, you look marvelous! Your mother could have been a costume designer. Okay, now the second-grade snowflakes, please . . ."

"Just a minute." It was Mrs. Sturdivant. "Do you think the bells might be a problem?"

I looked down at my jingling toes. Mom was so proud of finally getting those bells to dangle just so.

"Aren't they a bit distracting?" Mrs. Sturdivant said. "I'm concerned they might take attention away from the other characters."

Ha! That was a good one! As if my mother and I had conspired to hog the show! I glanced at Monica standing flat-footed in the wings, toe shoes turned out, arms crossed over her chest, sleeves puffed up as high as her ears. Mrs. Sturdivant had sewn a million little sparklies on that dress to make absolutely sure everybody looked at Monica and nobody else every minute she was onstage.

Ms. Carlotti flipped her pink and purple scarf back. "Oh, I can't see the bells being any problem." She zeroed in on her clipboard again, then looked toward the wings. "Wind-up toys?"

I spun to hurry off and nearly flattened a kid with a big foil key on his back.

Out in the hall, Orin Downard and his buddy Nathan were laying for me.

"Aw gee," Orin said. "He is just so darn cute!"

"Oh, shut up." A guy gets touchy, wearing baggy tights.

"Golly, he's in a bad mood," Nathan said. "You better watch out, Orin. These pointy-eared guys can play pretty rough."

I tried to walk past but they blocked my way.

"And I *should* be nice," Orin said. "Because after all, this poor kid has big worries. Didn't you know that?"

"No," Nathan said, all big-eyed and fake sympathetic. "What's the trouble?"

"Oh, he's vewy wowwied about his baby brudder's wittle wost wabbit."

"I am not! Now get out of my way."

I went in the dressing room and peeled out of my tights and tunic in record time. That Orin! Sometimes I felt like he had some stupid power over me. Could he make me deny anything, just by saying it like an insult?

Nyeah, nyeah! You like to read!

Do not!

Nyeah, nyeah! You want to be an artist!

Do not!

Nyeah, nyeah! You like Christmas!

Do not!

I thought about this as I bicycled home.

I thought about a lot of things, like Monica and her mother, how they loved to show off, and then how I didn't want my cousin Cassandra to see me in this costume. I thought about Jesse, too, having a nice time at home in front of his computer screen.

When I passed the turnoff to Homestead Road, I stopped for a moment, listening for Alfie, but all I heard was the wind in the tops of the fir trees.

Now, isn't it strange? They tell us God and Santa are always watching, and the postmaster says Alfie's got his binoculars trained on us too.

Personally, that's plenty of being watched for me. Who needs to be up on a stage in front of a million *more* eyes?

··12··

Fashion Dolls and Dancing Flappies

I banged open the front door. "I'm quitting the play!" I hollered.

"Whoa," Dad said, "for somebody who claims to hate theater, you're pretty darned dramatic." He and the kids were busily sticking different kinds of candy on a gingerbread house while, from the record player, Raffi belted out "Christmas Time's A-Coming."

The aroma of warm, spicy gingerbread drifted by my nose and I stopped, instantly falling under its spell.

"You've got more in the oven?" I asked.

"Of course!" Dad said. "Why stop when you're on a roll?"

"Look, Robby," Lucy said. "Dis our house."

"Yeah, I can tell." The fact that Dad always starts with a barn-patterned gingerbread pan helps, because our house did used to be a dairy barn. "Looks good, guys."

I surveyed the dishes of various candies and scooped up a handful of my favorites—red and green M&M's.

"You're not serious about quitting the play, are you?" Dad said. "With the performance only a week away? Think of all the people you'd be letting down."

I popped an M&M in my mouth. "You know how they always say you have to be true to yourself? Well, I can't be Elroy the Elf," I said, "and still be true to myself."

"Oh, yeah?" Dad squirted green frosting over an upside down ice cream cone to make a fir tree. "Well,

I guess you'll just have to be false to yourself this once."

"Da-ad."

"What about all those junior elves? The way they look up to you?"

Freddie stuck his finger in the frosting. "How many days till Christmas?"

"About ten," Dad said.

"Ten? Lucy! Ten more days!"

"Maybe it was a mistake," Dad said, turning back to me again, "but nobody made you try out, and you did make a commitment. So my advice is to grit your teeth and see this through."

"How would you like to show off your legs in baggy tights in front of a whole lot of people? And now they're making me wear pointy ears, too!"

"I wore a pig snout to the Halloween party last year."

"Yeah, but that was your own choice."

"True."

"And you goofed off to get out of playing the piano when you were my age."

"Yeah, well, I was a rotten kid, okay? Maybe our plan should be to improve our family a little bit each generation."

The truth is, I wasn't surprised he wouldn't let me quit. It did feel good to gripe about it, though.

Dad and I have this tradition of shopping for the local toy drive. We're supposed to think of others at Christmas, Dad says, and it's more fun to actually buy the gifts than donate money.

"But I thought we were broke this year," I told Dad.

"No, things aren't quite *that* bad. And there's plenty of people worse off than we are."

At the store, Dad stood Lucy in front of a big wall of dolls. He'd been saying how handy it would be to have the female viewpoint on choosing toys this year.

"See any you like?" he asked her.

Bewildered, Lucy cringed before a hundred grinning fashion dolls. She gave Dad a worried look. Then she backed away, easing sideways toward the troll dolls.

"That just shows she's smart, Dad," I said. "I don't know if you've ever noticed, but those Barbie dolls have very strange bodies."

Dad seemed to find this funny. "You think so, huh?"

"Yes! Get a baby doll if you have to get a doll. Something cuddly. Girls like those, I think."

Lucy, meanwhile, had picked a troll with duck yellow fuzz hair a lot like her own.

"Some kid would like a popper gun," Freddie said.

"Yes, some kid probably would," Dad said, "but we're not going to inflict that noise on some kid's poor parents. Anyway, guns are against the Christmas spirit."

When we had enough toy drive stuff, Dad said we ought to look for gifts for our cousins. We spent a long time at it. I guess it's true what he said the other night —it's not easy buying something for somebody you don't know that well.

We finally got a Lego pirate set for Cameron, which was my idea, and a diary for Cassandra, a nice one with a satin ribbon marker, gold flower designs stamped on the front, and a lock for privacy.

"It's a gamble, sure," Dad said. "She might never write in it. But if she does . . . well, your mom's got a diary she kept at that age, and I know she treasures it now."

As we headed for the cash register, the twins finally figured out the stuff in the cart wasn't for them.

"Dis *my* troll!" Lucy said.

"No, no, Honey." Dad pried it out of her grip. "Remember I explained we were picking these out for kids who might not get any presents?"

No, she didn't remember.

"Maybe they're too young for this," I told Dad, taking over on the cart pushing so he could deal with them.

"They'll learn," Dad said, calmly dragging a kicking Freddie away from the GI Joe display. "You were just three when I first started bringing you, and you caught on. Hey, by the—ow! Freddie, don't kick!—by the fourth toy drive, you hardly fussed at all!"

"I used to fuss?"

Dad rolled his eyes like he couldn't believe I didn't remember.

Well, I remember lots of discussions, and hearing about how it's more blessed to give than to receive and thinking, *Yeah, but receiving's more fun.* Had I pitched fits like this, though?

Freddie and Lucy were so cranked out they wouldn't even stop and sit on the store Santa's lap.

"But guys!" I kept saying. "Free candy canes!"

"We can pass on that," Dad said.

At the van, Dad asked who wanted to go through the car wash.

"I do! I do!" they cried, instantly cheered.

Actually, Dad doesn't give a darn whether the van is squeaky clean or caked in mud, but the kids think the car wash is the next best thing to a carnival ride, so we take it through every so often.

"Do-it-yourself or dancing flappies?" he asked, using the name Freddie gave the drive-through because of the rubber strips that wiggle and slap the windshield.

Freddie and Lucy hesitated, watching each other.

"Do-it-yourself!" Lucy blurted.

"No! Dancing flappies!"

They pull this all the time, one waiting to see what the other wants, just to argue the opposite.

"Lucy spoke first," Dad said, turning in at the Splish-Splash Auto Bath.

While the twins were fighting over who got to drop the quarters in the vacuum machine, a car pulled up in front of the bay next to us. It was Mrs. Van Gent, the school counselor.

Oh, brother.

Now, I don't really know why I say that. She's actually pretty nice, and when she's wearing a parka with sweatpants and running shoes like now, she isn't nearly so serious as she seems at school.

She saw me and waved. My face got hot. She'd see my dad acting silly now. Freddie and Lucy were bound to embarrass me too.

Sure enough, with the kids rolling around on the seats, Dad started vacuuming their tummies, making them shriek. I stood by the van and looked up at the gray sky to show disgust. If Mrs. Van Gent glanced over here, I wanted her to realize how totally immature I thought this was.

"Dad," I said, when the vacuum's roar died away, "can't we just vacuum the car like everyone else?"

Dad blinked. "I suppose we could." Then he grinned. "But what would be the point of that?" He handed Lucy a couple more quarters. "Your turn now, Honey."

A dollar's worth of vacuuming is Dad's limit whether the van gets clean or not, so when the machine died down the second time, he put the kids in and slid the van door shut. Leaving me out beside the coin slot and dials, he drove the van into the washing bay. Then he got out, signaled me to drop the first coins, and started racing the clock, scrubbing the van with the brush that spewed great globs of white foam. Next came the rinsing. Inside the van, the twins bounced around, screaming, thrilled at facing the water blasts through nothing but a sheet of window glass.

I was supposed to stand by the coin slot with a stack of quarters and feed in more if the warning light showed time was almost up. If you let the machine go off, you have to start all over with six quarters.

The first time that happened to us back when Mom was pregnant with the twins, Dad just said to heck with it if that's what happens when you try to do a thorough job, and we drove the van off all foamy. When we got home, Mom was so bugged, she turned on the garden hose full force and sprayed Dad right along with the van!

So mine was an important job. I stood there,

breathing in the sharp smell of foamy detergent, keeping my eyes glued to that light.

"Does your family come here a lot, Robby?" It was Mrs. Van Gent at my elbow.

"No, not really," I said. "Just when the kids get cranky."

She cocked her head, puzzled. "You know how it works, though? I've never done this."

So I explained all the different settings and stuff, feeling kind of grown-up. The main thing, I told her, was to hurry, because you only have so much time.

She started in with the usual beginner type problems—getting the hose twisted up, not being able to yank it around. And the wind kept gusting through, catching her in the spray.

She laughed and pushed her wet hair out of her face and shouted, "Next time, the drive-through for me!"

I watched her, amazed at how much long hair she had. You'd never guess it when it's all wadded up in a bun at school . . .

"Robby! Ding-dong it!"

Uh-oh. Our machine had stopped. I'd missed the light and Dad wasn't done.

"Sorry, Dad."

"Oh, well. I was almost finished. The rain'll take care of the rest of that." He winked. "And I'm safe. With your mom holed up in her studio all day, she won't be watching to get me with the hose."

"Dad. She wouldn't do that in the winter."

"You never know!"

Mrs. Van Gent was still trying to spray off the foam. Whoa! Her amber warning light was flashing and she wasn't even noticing! I scooped our unused quarters off the ledge and dashed over to feed in the coins.

"Oh, thanks!" she called over the spray's roar, flashing a big smile at me.

I blushed, wanting to grin. I felt good about it, all the way home.

Even if I *was* riding in a streaky car myself.

·13·

Home Alone

"Are you sure you'll be okay, Robby?" Mom said. She and Dad were stuffing the twins into their jackets, getting ready to haul them along to Douglas Bay for more shopping.

"Beth, he'll be fine."

"I'll be fine," I echoed Dad. This was a first, me being allowed to stay behind. I lay under the Christmas tree, gazing up through the branches at the blinking lights and Styrofoam peanut chains.

"Dial nine one one if there's an emergency."

"Right, Mom."

"How many days till Christmas?" Freddie said.

"Uh . . ." Dad zipped his jacket. "Nine."

"Don't open the door to strangers," Mom said.

"Right, Mom." I don't think there has ever once been a stranger at our door up here on this road.

"Don't open the door for the gorilla man," Freddie said.

"What?" I flashed on Bigfoot, wondering for an instant if Freddie knew something I didn't.

"The tax man," he explained, "is a gorilla."

Mom was looking at me while talking to Dad. "Is there anything else we ought to be telling Robby?"

"Yeah," Dad said, herding Freddie and Lucy out. "How about good-bye?"

As soon as I heard the minivan bump over the plank bridge, I rolled out from under the tree and went to the window. I turned and scanned the empty room. Well, maybe *empty*'s not the right word, what with a lineup of stuffed animals tricked out as Santa's reindeer ringing the Christmas tree.

But it was awfully quiet.

I drifted all through the house, upstairs and down, just to see what it felt like, being here by myself. *Too* quiet, I decided. I would put on a record.

We have three kinds of Christmas records. First, the kid stuff. Then there's Dad's jazz-'em-up Cajun albums and Mom's calm-'em-down guitars and music boxes. I wanted something cheery so I went for Dad's.

It's a funny thing about Cajun music. If you don't understand the French words, you'd think they were happy songs. But read the translations on the album covers—they're about these French Catholics getting kicked out of Acadia, up in Canada, and running away to Louisiana. Boy, every time you turn around it's another story about people hassling each other over religion . . .

Anyway, I put on "Christmas Bayou" and got to work. This was my chance to get my gifts wrapped. I climbed up to my loft and brought them down.

For Dad I'd sent away for a record album with a guy

playing the accordion on the front—"Da' Big Squeeze —Roddie Romero and the Rockin' Cajuns." For my mom, a bottle of strawberry bubble bath and three sets of Day-Glo green spongy earplugs. At my favorite bookstore in Douglas Bay, the saleslady helped me find Lucy a giant panda book. She's nuts about pandas, see, and already talks about going to China when she grows up to help save them from extinction.

And for Freddie—well, it was a long shot, but with no calls coming on my lost bunny poster, I decided to try getting him a new bunny, a soft, squishy Peter Rabbit with a blue velvet coat and a pinkish felt carrot. I hoped he wouldn't feel insulted. A new rabbit could never replace Buddy, but maybe he'd start to love this one after a while.

Funny—I couldn't even remember what I'd given Freddie and Lucy last year, probably because Mom and Dad had pretty much steered me through the shopping, with me just saying "Sure, whatever you think."

But now, getting the wrapping paper and ribbon from the hall closet, I was feeling good at imagining how much each person was going to like what I'd bought them. Giving was turning out to be more fun than I used to think.

Still, there's a lot to be said for receiving. So what *was* I going to get? The running shoes? The rubber raft? I'd asked for one I could use in the summer, down where Nekomah Creek makes a big pool on the beach.

When I had the presents all wrapped, I considered putting them under the tree, then thought better of it. The presents from my cousins had been there for a while, and the twins had shaken and fiddled with them until the paper started to get torn. Finally Mom stuck them on the top shelf of the hall closet.

"I should know better than to trust the twins yet, anyway," she said to me. "You remember your two-year birthday party."

She always tells how I got up from my nap, sneaked down and opened all my piled up presents while she and Dad were out crepe papering the yard. I didn't get in trouble, though. She said I was too young to know any better.

Now, when I went to put my presents on the top shelf, I was amazed how stuffed with other gifts it was. I stood there looking over all the red, green, and foil-wrapped gifts.

I spotted my package from California. Boy, wouldn't it be nice to know what it was? That way I could make up the right thing to say in advance.

A little thought popped into my head. Why not just check it out? I could open it, take a peek, and wrap it back up. My wrapping was pretty good now— I'll bet no one would ever know.

I dragged a chair down the hall, climbed up on it and pulled out the box, my heart thudding. I carried it to the kitchen table.

Then I went out on the porch to listen for the minivan. It was way too soon for them to come back, but in our family, shopping trips sometimes get cut short if somebody throws up or even just gets so fussy Mom and Dad can't stand it anymore.

I listened. Nothing but the wind rushing through fir boughs.

Okay, go for it. I slipped back in and started trying

to oh-so-carefully unpeel the Scotch tape. So far so good. Next I slid the white box out. I lifted the lid and reached into the tissue paper.

Aaauuuggghhh! Neon green and pink shorts in a zigzag pattern, the bottoms banded with purple polka dots!

I mashed them back into the tissue. My heart pounded as I rewrapped the package and scuttled down the hall. I climbed up and shoved it back into the closet. Finally I hauled the telltale chair back to the kitchen.

Whew! Made it. I fell on the sofa, panting like I'd just run a mile with Bigfoot chasing me.

Gee, I thought when I'd calmed down, I sure hope the rest of my presents aren't that bad. I dangled my arm, picking at a loose thread in the braid rug. If only I could be sure I had at least one decent present coming, I'd probably feel a whole lot better.

Just one.

I sat up. Before I could think about it too hard, I grabbed the chair and made a second beeline for the treasure trove closet. I hesitated just an instant, then yanked out packages until I found one tagged to me from Mom and Dad. I hurried into the kitchen with it. Thud thud thud. My heart hurt. Another porch check —no sign of the van.

I hurried back in. Carefully, quickly, I opened the package. Yeah, okay, it was a couple of books I wanted. I rewrapped it, shoved it back into place on the shelf.

I stood in the hall with an odd, sinking feeling. "Christmas Bayou" had long since finished and the record chick-chick-chicked through the speaker. Maybe the next package would somehow be more of a thrill?

Well, there's no getting around what I did. It was a heart-hammering, half-hour orgy. Unwrap it. Check it out. Wrap it back up. Unwrap it. Check it out. Wrap it back up. I didn't stop until I'd looked at every single one of my presents, including the big one I found in the back—the rubber raft.

Afterward, I put on a record of calming, innocent-sounding Christmas music. Okay, I thought, sitting on the sofa, waiting for Mom and Dad to come back. Okay. I'm getting almost everything I want.

So how come I felt so weird? Was it because there weren't any running shoes? Was it just the Sunday afternoon blahs?

And where was everybody? I jumped up. It was too darned quiet around here.

I went out on the porch. That's when I heard it— Alfie's voice, moaning over the treetops.

This is dumb, I know. But I tore back inside, shut the door and locked it, breathing hard. Hadn't my heart pounded more than enough for one day already?

·:14:·

A Shock

Calm and confident, Jesse stood in front of our class in his green Dartmouth College sweatshirt and unfolded one elaborate chart after another for his ocean pollution report. He had computer-generated data and graphs made on a color printer—all very professional-looking.

"Aw, his dad musta did the whole thing," Orin muttered.

I'd have thought that too except you could tell Jesse knew exactly what he was talking about. He explained the big words and gave examples everyone could understand. I glanced around. People looked dazed. How could he remember so much?

My heart sank by degrees as he went on. I was probably up next. What an act to follow!

Not that I wasn't proud of my dough model, of course. It's not easy to make a whole miniature forest out of twigs and moss and stuff. I had cute, happy clay

animals glued on the healthy-stream side, and a lot of
dead and disgusted-looking ones on the other. But it
had been sitting there on the table by the window for
two days now and everybody'd already had a chance
to look at it. What was I supposed to say about it now?
Duh! Note the dead fish. That'd be great.

Turned out Ben was next, though. He talked about
global warming. Yes, it's a problem, he said, but don't
blame the cows. He proudly concluded with a recent
study by two Cornell University economists who said
that one 75-watt light bulb operating for a year had as
much warming effect as a single cow.

"If everyone changed to fluorescent lights," Ben
said, "it would help more than worrying about cow
. . . um . . . emissions. And here in Tillamook
County, we really need our cows!"

"Yes!" several people burst out.

"Mooooo!" a bunch more joined in.

I would have been glad for the cow cheer to go on
forever, but finally it died down, and Ms. Carlotti said
it was my turn.

My knees felt weak as I made my way to the front. I
looked at all the faces watching me, waiting. I swallowed hard. My lips were stuck to my teeth. Boy, if
getting up in front of my own class was this bad, what
was going to happen when I walked out on that stage
for the play?

"Go ahead, Robby," Ms. Carlotti said.

I started floundering around about how destructive
it is for fish habitat when you cut down the trees by
the streams.

"Without shade, the water gets too warm," I explained. "Plus, without the tree roots, mud washes into the water. Fish don't like that."

I stood there, my mind blank. In the quiet I heard Orin start up a little singsong: "Elroy, the Christmas Elf . . ."

"Class," Ms. Carlotti said, staring straight at Orin. She turned back to me. "And what might some solutions be, Robby?"

"Uh . . . well, you need laws about not cutting the trees too close to the stream. And people have to follow the laws." Think. *Think*. I'd read lots more about it than that. . . . "Uh . . . you can . . . uh . . . take a closer look at my model sometime. If you want." *How lame!*

"Okay. Well, you certainly did a nice job on the model, Robby. Your artwork is always marvelous. Any questions, class?"

Jesse spoke right up, "I'm curious, Mr. Hummer," he said, sounding like an important news reporter. "What prompted you to use Xs for the eyes of the dead fish? That is to say, what is the deeper significance here?"

"Jesse." I blushed furiously while everyone, including Ms. Carlotti, had a good laugh. I wasn't really mad, though. Jesse never hassled anyone who wasn't his buddy. "I got it from comic strips, okay? Everybody knows those Xs for eyes mean dead. Or at least seriously beat up, okay? *Mr. Glenn.*"

With play rehearsals almost every day, it had been a long time since I'd been able to go home with Jesse after school, and I was feeling happy as I followed him onto his school bus that afternoon.

"So what did you get on your report?" I asked, dropping into a seat beside him.

"An A."

"Figures. I got a B. Actually, that's pretty good, considering I forgot half of what I meant to say."

"I thought you did okay," Jesse said, but he was just being nice.

I knew I'd lost it, standing up there in front of everyone. What if I did that in the play?

Well, I thought as Breanna passed our seat, at least my report wasn't as boring as hers. Her mom got her excused from the real environmental problems assignment, and for a substitute report, all she did was tell the scientific names of different wildflowers. Made a pretty chart, but what's to think about?

"Let me see your notebook," Jesse said. He always likes to check out the latest doodles on the cover. Lately I'd been doing lots of 3-D science fiction vehicles. "Cool," he said.

When we passed the sign for Homestead Road, I leaned toward him and lowered my voice. "Up there's where an old hermit lives."

"Really?"

"Yeah. Kind of a spooky guy. He gets up on his roof and lets out these bloodcurdling cries."

Jesse's brown eyes got big.

I hesitated. When you have someone's attention like that, you naturally want to keep it. But was passing on Monica's stories really fair? Even using the word *bloodcurdling* for Alfie's hymn singing was kind of an exaggeration. "I saw him at the post office last week," I said, sticking to the facts. "He didn't look like a wild man or anything."

"Yeah?" Jesse said, but now without the same interest.

Because, after all, how mysterious could a hermit be if people could see him at the post office?

I settled back into my seat. I guess the truth usually isn't as intriguing as a lie. Maybe that's why lies get around so much easier.

Jesse talked for a while about the new computer game he wanted for Christmas; then he said, "So what are you asking for?"

"Uh . . ." Since I'd already opened all my presents, this was an awkward question. Boy, if I'd known how the guilt was going to get to me, I'd have stayed out of that closet! I wondered what Jesse would say if I told him what I'd done.

"Come on," Jesse said. "You must have asked for *something*."

"Yeah, sure. A rubber raft."

"Cool."

I nodded. "I hope you'll be here for at least part of the summer so you can take it down on the beach with me." I caught myself. "I mean, *if* I get it."

"Sure. Great."

I thought about my other presents—the books, and the pink and green shorts that had been haunting me. Would Jesse wear that sort of thing?

As we turned onto Highway 101, voices rose behind us. I craned around. Breanna Holter's older brother was arguing with another eighth grader.

"No way!"

"Yes sir."

"Oh, you're all so full of it!"

"They have this fight at least once a week," Jesse

whispered. "It's that bunch from Breanna Holter's church. Those other guys just love to get 'em going about people burning in hell."

"That whole thing is so dumb," I said. "I know lots of good dead people who never went to Breanna's church."

Jesse smiled. "Good dead people?"

"You know what I mean. People I just *know* never went to hell. Don't you?"

Jesse's copper-colored eyebrows went together. "I don't think about heaven or hell in the first place. I don't believe in any of it. I don't even believe in God."

For a moment I thought I hadn't heard right. The words hung like a puff of cold between us. I stared at his white running shoes, braced on the back of the next seat. I swallowed, getting my voice ready to come out normal sounding.

"You don't believe in God at all?"

"Nah."

I sank down and looked past him, out the window. A while later, after we'd turned up his road, I said, "Why don't you?"

"Why don't I what?"

"Believe in God."

"Oh. Well, for one thing, like my dad says, you can't prove it. And for another, just look at the mess the world's in. If there was a God, how could he let little kids starve and get killed in wars?"

The bus stopped. I let Jesse out of the seat and followed him off the bus.

We started up the gravel drive to his house.

"If you don't believe in God," I said, "how do you celebrate Christmas?"

"Duh!" He grinned. "With a tree and presents like everybody else, of course. The presents are the best part anyway, right?"

"Yeah, I guess." But Christmas wasn't the big question anyway. The real question was one I was afraid to ask. If he didn't believe in God, what did he think happens to us when we die?

We went in and got a snack. I wasn't that hungry, though. Then we parked ourselves in front of his computer screen.

I couldn't tell you now what we played that afternoon. My eyes watched the figures zip around the screen but I was stuck on Jesse's announcement. He flat-out didn't believe in God. And I could tell he hadn't said it just to be daring either. He'd already forgotten it.

But I couldn't.

It was easy to think of good people who couldn't possibly have gone to hell like Breanna said, but it was harder to deny Jesse's reasoning about all the terrible things happening in the world. Right that minute I could hear more of it pouring into Jesse's house through the TV his mom had on in the kitchen. Even my dad admitted the world was a mess with wars and famines. Why would God let those things happen?

When Jesse's mom said she could either drive me back to Nekomah Creek before dinner or after, I chose before. Somehow I wanted to be at home.

When I got there, though, the place was a madhouse. A strange four-wheel drive was parked in the driveway and Mom said the IRS guy was up in the guest room, working on the audit.

"And he can't eat cookies!" Lucy said.

"Huh?"

"Isn't that funny?" Mom said. "The kids tried to take him some and he told them IRS rules forbid accepting food because it might be seen as a bribe!"

"But he's not a gorilla," Lucy added.

"No, no, he's perfectly nice," Mom said. "Now let's check out the sofa bed. We'll have Cassandra sleep here."

She kicked toys away from the sofa under the window, tossed off the cushions, and pulled up the folding mechanism. The instant the braces hit the floor, the twins were up jumping on the mattress.

"Hey, look," I said, "here's that slingshot we lost."

"I'll take that," Mom said with a deft swipe.

"And my Silly Putty!" I pulled it up. It was stuck full of lint.

"Mommy," Freddie said, "how many days till Christmas?"

The phone rang as the IRS man appeared at the second-floor balcony, a little guy with a salt-and-pepper beard and a red plaid tie. A funny thought popped into my head. *He* should have been playing Elroy the Elf.

"Mrs. Hummer? Could you come up and answer a few questions for me?"

Mom put her hand over the phone. "Be right there." She spoke into the receiver. "I'll have to call you back." She headed for the stairs. "Robby, tell Daddy to come in from the workshop. There's just—

well, this is *his* brother who's coming tomorrow and—
Lucy, get *down* from there!"

In his workshop, Dad saw me and pushed back his safety goggles.

"Dad? When I was over at Jesse's, he said—"

"Bi—ill!" It was Mom, hollering.

I sighed. "You better go in, Dad. The tax guy just called Mom up to answer a bunch of questions. I think there's something wrong."

"Oh, I doubt it. We've both been running up and down the stairs answering questions all day." He slapped the sawdust off his thighs. "You know, Robby, I don't envy that guy his job. Nobody's ever happy to have the IRS around."

"Daddy!" the twins yelled as we came in. "Daddy, watch this!"

"Bill?" Mom called.

"For joy! For joy!" The kids bounced on the fold-out bed. "It's great to be a toy . . . !"

It was hours before things had calmed down to where a person could string two sentences together. While Dad was serenading the kids in the bathtub with his accordion, I went back to the bedroom where Mom was folding clothes.

"Mom? You know what Jesse said today? He said he doesn't believe in God."

"Oh?" She stopped folding for just an instant, then continued.

"Neither do his parents."

"Yes, well . . ."

I waited. "You don't sound very shocked."

She put a towel on a stack. "Should I be? I'm sure lots of people don't believe in God."

"But—"

Now *she* waited. "But what?"

"Well, his parents are really smart scientists."

She let a towel drop back into the basket and sat down on the edge of the bed.

"Jesse's smart too," I said.

She looked at me. "So this really bothers you."

"Well, yeah. I mean, Breanna's burning-in-hell stuff bugs me, but the idea of no God and no . . . well, no *plan* about the universe or anything . . . that's worse."

She nodded. "I had a friend like Jesse once. I thought she knew everything. When she said she didn't believe in God, I was crushed. When she went off to college, she gave me a box of all her old trinkets and beads, including a gold cross with her name engraved on it. She said it didn't mean anything to her anymore. Well, I hung on to that cross for years. And then you know what?"

"What?"

"She became a minister! I sent it back to her as an ordination gift."

"She became a minister even though she didn't believe in God?"

"No, no, later she *did*. That's the point. People grow and sometimes change their minds. In fact, this is something most of us spend our whole lives trying to work out."

"What if Jesse doesn't change his mind?"

"Then he doesn't. That's his business. It doesn't mean you can't believe what *you* believe."

I let myself flop into the pile of warm-from-the-drier towels on the bed. I turned my face to the side. "Jesse says how could a God let so many bad things happen?"

"Oh, sweetheart . . ." I felt her hand on my back. "I'm sure that's something people have been wondering about since day one." She sighed. "I wish I had a good answer for you."

"But you don't."

"No, I don't."

·· 15 ··

Yippee-ki-yi-yay!

"Maybe the plane will be late," I said, coming in from school on Friday afternoon. It was countdown until curtain on the play that night.

"Tough luck," Mom said. "Uncle Fred already called from the airport. They're on their way."

Well, there's always the consolation of cookies.

"Are these up for grabs?" I said, checking out the plates of different kinds she had all over the counter.

"These." She pushed forward the one with broken bits. "The others are for the mailman, the paperlady, and the preschool teachers." She poured herself a cup of coffee, took a chunk of gingerbread man, and sank down at the kitchen table with a sigh. "Just the thought of your dad and his brother getting together exhausts me. You know how they act."

I grinned. "Yeah." That part of the visit would be fun anyway. Mom says Dad and my uncles always revert to their childhoods when they see each other.

Cameron wasn't the only one going crazy with the popper gun last time we got together.

"And then your aunt Pat. Her housekeeping standards are so much higher than mine. When we took you down for that last visit, your dad and I wore ourselves out, trying to keep you reined in. We even left a couple of days early."

"We did?" Mostly what I remembered about Aunt Pat was how she had all these thick, perfumey magazines that were perfect for teaching Cameron how to erase the fancy ladies' eyeballs and black out their teeth.

"I used to have standards." Mom rested her chin on her hand and gazed across to the living room. "But that was long ago in a galaxy far, far away . . ."

"Mom? About the play? I honestly, sincerely do not think Cassandra and Cameron would like it very much."

She looked toward the stairs. "I wish he'd finish up with that audit."

"I wish it was tomorrow," I said, "with the play already over." (If you get the feeling I was saying this a lot, you're right.)

"Well," Mom said wearily, "by tomorrow it will be, whatever happens."

I waited for her to tell me it was going to be fine and I was going to be great, but she didn't.

"I've been thinking," I said. "You know that tradition of saying 'Break a leg' before a performance? Maybe it was made up by kids who really thought it would be good luck to break a leg and not have to go through with their play."

"Oh, Robby . . ."

"Cassandra's probably going to make fun of me. They probably do grown-up plays at her school."

"I doubt that. She's not that much older than you."

"Mom, do you ever check out the seventh-grade girls at Nekomah Creek? They look like grown-ups. They—"

Banging noises from upstairs.

"What was that?" Mom said.

"Ow! Why, you little—"

"It's the tax man," I whispered.

Mom started up the stairs. I followed, Lucy and Freddie suddenly on my heels, spilling from their closet fort like they could smell trouble and wanted in on it.

"Mr. Wirfs?" Mom said through the closed door.

Bam! Was he pounding the card table with his fist? Mom and I looked at each other.

The door flew open.

"Ants!" he cried. "All over the place in here. *Biting* ants."

"Oh, no," Mom said.

He waved his arms over the table. "I have been in hundreds of homes, but I have never—" Bam! His fist came down again.

Mom fell to her hands and knees, trying to catch the little black critters that were scurrying away from the plastic ant farm in all directions.

Lucy and Freddie stood there, big-eyed.

Bam! The tax man nailed another.

Lucy shrieked.

"Don't you dare!" I said. "Don't you dare kill my dad's ants!"

"Well, I'm sorry, but . . . Excuse me." He pushed past, heading for the bathroom, pulling at the seat of his pants.

"I can't believe this," Mom said. "How did they get out? Robby, hurry! Get a paper cup or something."

I skipped down the stairs. Wow! Me, Robby Hummer, standing up to the IRS! Dad was just coming in the back.

"Dad! The ants are loose! They're running all over, biting the tax guy."

We hurried up the stairs and passed out cups. All five of us were crawling around on the floor trying to scoop ants when Mr. Wirfs reappeared at the door.

"Hey, sorry about this," Dad said.

Mr. Wirfs reached over us and scooped up the papers on the card table and stuffed them into his briefcase. "I'm quite close to finishing," he said. "I believe I can clear up any final questions over the phone."

"Oh, really?" Dad said. "Well, fine." He stood.

"No, no, please. I'll show myself out. I think you should stay right here and . . . corral your ants."

But Mom followed him into the hall. "You really must take some cookies," I heard her say.

"Oh, no."

"But it's not a bribe. Just to even things up . . ."

"Rules are rules," he said.

"Well, if you won't let us feed you cookies, I hope you won't penalize us for the ants."

He laughed, which surprised me. "Everything seems to be in order, Mrs. Hummer. Well, perhaps that's a poor choice of words. Put it this way: I didn't find any major problems."

"*That's* good to know."

"And actually, although I'm not really supposed to say anything at this point, it looks to me as if the IRS may owe *you*."

"Really?"

"Yes, I found a math error to the tune of seven hundred dollars."

"Did you hear that?" Mom said when he'd gone. "We're getting money back! Seven hundred dollars."

"Ouch!" Dad said. "That's great, but—"

"Oh, no!" Mom hit the floor again. "Here's a couple more ants clear over by the bed. We're never going to get them all."

"Whoa, boys!" I said. "A stray."

"Herd him on over here," Dad said. "Wait a minute. Did you say seven hundred?"

Well, I swear, it was like somebody flipped the silly switch. He jumped up and started belting out some old cattle-drive song in a hokey tough-guy voice. "Git along, little dogies!" He bow-legged cowboy-style around the room and pounced on an ant. Holding it in the palm of his hand, he struggled and cussed—*dad gummit!*—pretending to rope, throw, and brand that tiny dogie until he had the twins screaming with laughter and me clutching my guts in helpless hysteria.

"Dad, stop! My stomach!" I pleaded, but my giggling just egged him on.

"Yippee-ki-yi-yay!" He sang until he ran out of words and then he started making them up, throwing in stuff about Santa Claus and IRS money and the chorus of "Cielito Lindo."

"*Ay, ay, ay, ay! Canta y no llores!*"

Laughing with us now, Mom forgot the ants and let Dad pull her up.

"Mommy?" Lucy said, startled to see our own mother tear into a rip-roaring Spanish-style dance, stamping and snapping her fingers, her cheeks flushed.

> *Ay, ay, ay, ay!*
> *Sing and don't cry!*
> *The ants are loose in the guest room*
> *And the tax man, he says bye-bye!*

Dad spun Mom and dipped her backward till her hair swept the floor, and that's the pose they were holding when we heard Uncle Fred's voice downstairs.

"Yo! We're here! Anybody home?"

Mom and Dad bugged eyes at each other.

"Come on in!" Dad yelled even though obviously they already had.

He stood Mom unsteadily on her feet as the twins scampered past, and finally all five of us were assembled on the second-floor balcony.

"Well, hel-loo!" Mom sang breathlessly. "We were just . . . ah . . . getting the guest room ready!"

·:16:·

Break a Leg

Cassandra and Cameron stood in the door in front of their parents, staring at our Christmas tree.

"Check *that*!" Cameron said.

Cassandra looked nothing like the frilly girl in the picture. Her hair wasn't fluffy at all, but sleeked back into a braid. The very first thing she did was dive into a forward roll across our rug, standing up with a snap.

"Cassandra!" Aunt Pat said.

But I thought it was neat. You have to like a girl who makes an entrance with a somersault.

She smiled at me. "Aikido."

"Huh?"

"Sort of like judo. Or karate." She executed an equally stylish backward roll.

"She does this all the time," Aunt Pat said. "Makes the whole house shake."

"Well!" Dad clapped his hands in that *get ready* sort

of way. "Now she can make *our* house shake for a while."

Within minutes all us kids were trying it.

Here's something I've noticed: The things I really look forward to often don't turn out as great as I'm imagining. On the other hand, the things I most dread are never as bad as I'm thinking, either.

That's how it was with Cass, as she called herself now. She was nice. She was even interested in the play.

"Aren't you excited?" she said as she helped me set the dinner table.

"No," I said. "I'm dreading it."

" 'Cause you're nervous about forgetting your lines and stuff?"

"Not really. I know my lines. I just hate having all those people looking at me."

"But that's what they're supposed to be doing. And if they're liking it, wouldn't that make you feel good?"

I stopped dealing plates for a moment. "I guess I never picture them liking it."

"What *do* you picture? People throwing rotten to-matoes?"

I couldn't help grinning. We must have grown up on the same cartoons.

"What you need is to play 'the worst that could happen,' " Cass said.

"Huh?"

"What would it be? The worst thing while you're onstage."

I thought. I would forget my lines and blow it? I

would trip and fall? People would laugh at me? My mother would give me the exact opposite of a glowy look? Jesse would shake his head over my idiocy?

"There's this kid named Orin Downard," I told Cass. "Wouldn't surprise me if he got me with a peashooter. That would be pretty bad."

"Come on. Nobody's going to let him get away with that."

"He's been threatening me all through rehearsals."

"Probably just jealous. I know I would be. Our school did a play but I didn't get a part at all. Not even a little one. And my mom says you have one of the biggest parts of all."

"Yeah. I have this big long speech at the end."

"Well, Robby, you ought to feel honored to have a lead role."

"Yeah?" Funny. This is the same thing all the grown-ups had been telling me, but when Cass said it, somehow I was more willing to believe it.

After dinner, which I couldn't eat, Mom drove me up to the school. People in the play needed a whole hour to get dressed and put on makeup.

The air in the back hall was thick with the smell of greasepaint and powder. Kids were saying their lines a mile a minute.

"Go out and be wonderful!" Ms. Carlotti said as we gathered for her final pep talk. She flung back the fanciest scarf I'd seen her wear yet—one with swirls of real gold. The man with her gave her shoulders a squeeze. I blinked. Must be her husband. I'm always forgetting that teachers have lives outside school.

"Now, what do we tell each other?" she concluded.

"Break a leg!" we all cried back.

In a swarm of giggling, whispering toys and elves, I climbed the back stairs to the stage. Out front we could hear the dull roar of the audience. The place must be packed.

"Quiet, quiet!" Ms. Carlotti whispered. "Here we go!" She switched on the taped introduction music.

I had listened to that music dozens of times. But tonight, knowing there was an audience, it sounded different. This must be the opening night excitement Mom was always talking about.

I peeked out the crack of the curtains. Was Orin out there somewhere? "Tonight's the big night," he'd said to me with a sneer at school that day. "I can't wait."

Hey, my family was in the front row! Freddie and Lucy were standing on their seats, all but jumping up and down, and Cass and Cameron looked kind of excited too.

Dad and Uncle Fred were talking, but Aunt Pat looked like a person who would really rather be somewhere else. Maybe she was still sore about that ant bite. Oh, well . . .

Next I checked Mom. She gazed up at the closed curtains, over at Aunt Pat, then glanced at her watch. She seemed . . . *worried*. Gee. Maybe my fretting and complaining had really gotten to her.

Ms. Carlotti motioned back those of us who were peeking and, a moment later, the curtains opened with a swish.

I'll never forget that first time I walked out on the stage. I was standing in the light, but the audience had become a big, black pit of breathing, laughing, coughing beings, faceless except for the first few rows.

I felt stunned for a moment, then I started saying my lines.

Hey, that was *my* voice filling the auditorium! I spoke up louder, then made my exit with the toss of magical glitter that only the Head Elf got to throw.

From the wings I looked back onto the stage, breathing hard. I made it! I went out there and I survived!

During the dancing toy scene I put an eye to the curtain crack again. Freddie and Lucy were thrilled to see this number happening right in front of their eyes. "For joy! For joy! It's great to be a toy!" Freddie looked as if he would have jumped up onstage with them if anybody gave him a chance.

I scanned the audience. They were loving it. Their upturned faces reminded me of something. Oh, yeah —the crowd at the kids' Thanksgiving pageant. I saw now that our parents didn't care if the play was dumb. They just wanted to see us, their kids, up on the stage. We were older and not as cute as the preschoolers, but we were still their kids, and they were gazing up at us with those same glowy looks. I'll bet we could have recited the school hot lunch menu and they'd have looked just the same.

At least one part of the play wasn't dumb at all, though—Monica's dance solo. Yes, it kills me to admit this, and when she came off I knew she'd still be snippy Monica Sturdivant. But for a magic moment out there, spinning on her toes, sparkling in the light . . . well, I noticed I was holding my breath and I thought, *Oh, so this is what they mean by breathtaking.* And I thought how it was really kind of lucky for the rest of us that she *was* a show-off.

When it was my turn, I delivered my true-spirit-of-Christmas speech better than I ever had before. As the curtain closed, the audience clapped and cheered and we all took a million bows.

In the back hall mob afterward, I heard a lot of people fussing about me to my parents.

"How did he ever remember all those lines?" is what they mostly said.

My mother stood there pink and smiley. I saw Mrs. Van Gent and her husband talking to her and Dad, all of them glancing over at me. My neck got hot. I looked away.

I spotted Orin at the edge of the crowd. He made a

face but I just grinned at him. Too late for peashooters now. And he could hardly make fun of something his own parents thought was terrific. I watched his dad lift Peggy the snowflake up for a hug. Gee. Mr. Downard usually acts so rough and tough. I didn't know he had it in him to get all mushy over his little girl. And right out in public too. I wondered if Orin was wishing now he'd tried out himself.

Freddie and Lucy tugged on my arms but Cass and Cameron hung back like I had been transformed into somebody special.

Okay, I could see how people might get to liking this, how maybe they'd feel all the work and worrying that led up to the show were worth it. Still, I'm talking about other people. Not me. People like Freddie, for instance. He's such a ham.

A gray-haired lady my parents know came up and started clucking over him.

"What a darling little fellow," she said in a kootchy-koo voice. She bent down and put her face next to his. "Can you tell me, sweetie, what Santa says?"

"Sure!" Freddie put a hand over his chest and flung out the other. "Fare-WEELLL . . . my merry little elves . . ."

The woman blinked, delighted. "For land sakes!"

"Mom?" I whispered as we followed the others across the parking lot to the minivan.

"Yes?"

"Well . . . you looked so happy in there."

"Of course I'm happy. I'm very proud of you!"

"But Mom? Well, is it going to, like, break your heart if I don't ever do any more plays?"

"Ha!" She started laughing. "After what you put us through for the past three weeks?"

"Well, gee, I—"

"Robby, if you ever come home talking about trying out for another play, I will probably forbid it!"

"Oh."

She gave me a supersweet smile.

Parents are so weird.

·· 17 ··

Blazing Fingers

When we got home from the play, we kids climbed up into my loft, fluffing it into a cozy nest with piles of extra quilts. Instead of a popper gun, Cameron had brought his Game Boy, which he was being surprisingly nice about sharing, and the twins had taken to Cassandra like she was their long-lost big sister.

Below us, the grown-ups kicked off their shoes and pulled up around the wood stove, completely ignoring the fact that it was way past the twins' bedtime.

"Well, I'm not sorry *that's* over with," Mom said. "I hope I learned my lesson."

Funny, I never thought of grown-ups having to learn lessons. What had she learned?

"My turn," Lucy said, grabbing for the Game Boy.

I passed it without arguing, being in a generous mood. Just think—I would never, ever in my life have to dress up like an elf again!

"Freddie," I said, "don't you feel silly in those elf

boots?'' Cassandra had cinched them to his ankles with a couple of her hair dealies.

"No!" He kicked, shaking the toe bells for all he was worth. You could tell he loved having company to be his audience. Maybe it had even helped him forget Buddy Wabbit. He hadn't been sucking his finger anyway.

From downstairs, I could hear Mom and Dad telling about the tax man and how they were lucking out with a refund. Then Dad whispered something that made them all laugh.

"Your dad's kind of goofy, isn't he?" Cass said.

I nodded happily. The only thing nicer than being in a good mood yourself is having your parents in a good mood.

"Hey, Cass. Did you ever hear about this? One time when our dads were kids they were playing gunfighters with baseball bats for rifles. Their playhouse had real windows, see, and Dad got so excited, chasing and shooting, that he did like in the movies—just knocked out a pane of glass with the bat so he could keep on shooting!"

Cass's jaw dropped. "He did not!"

I sucked a breath. "Did too!"

"No, si-ir. It was *our* dad who did that."

What!

"Dad!" I hollered down through the slats. "Tell Cass how you did too knock out the playhouse window that time."

Four faces turned up to us.

"Now wait just a minute," Uncle Fred said to Dad. "*I* broke the playhouse window."

"Oh, yeah?" Dad straightened from his slouch. "Then how come *I* got paddled for it?"

"No, no, no," Uncle Fred said. "I got my allowance docked. You probably got paddled for something else."

"Oh, I love this," Mom said to Aunt Pat. "I'll bet at the time they were falling all over themselves claiming they *didn't* do it."

"Well, I've been telling my kids this story for years," Dad said.

"So have I!"

Slowly, ominously, Dad pushed up off the sofa.

Gee, I thought. It wasn't *that* big of a deal.

Dad stood, legs spread wide, hands open at his sides. "Well, pardner," he drawled, "I guess this story jest ain't big enough for the both of us."

Uncle Fred rose to face him, eyes narrowed. They drew. Pa-pow!

"Oh, Fred, *really*!" Aunt Pat looked at the ceiling.

The chase was on—over the sofas, up and down the stairs, they pa-powpowpowed each other.

"Dad!" I yelled. "Don't forget what you said! Guns are against the Christmas spirit!"

"These aren't guns!" Dad yelled back. "These are fingers!"

From the loft, we screamed and cheered, each bunch rooting for their own dad. Uncle Fred tackled Dad and they fell, rolling across the floor together.

"Come on!" I called to Freddie and Lucy, and we scrambled down the ladder to mix it up in the free-for-all.

"Cowabunga!" Cameron yelled, and Cass somersaulted into the pile of wrestling people.

"Look out for the tree!" Mom cried.

Well, it was one of those times, you know? It's night, and everyone's running around all wild, hot and panting and out of breath and it's just so much fun that you think of that expression "having the time of your life" and decide that, yeah, this must be what they mean.

We didn't quit until everyone was exhausted.

Dad ended up on the floor with Uncle Fred sitting on him.

"Robby," he said, "let this—oof!—be a lesson for you. Be nice to younger brothers when they're small. You never know—oof!—how big they might get in the end!"

"Gotcha, Dad." But I couldn't imagine Freddie ever getting bigger than me, or us kids being grown-ups together.

"I shudder to think," Mom said, giving Dad a hand up, "what would happen if we ever managed to get all of you Hummer boys in the same room together again."

"It's certainly not going to happen in any room of mine," Aunt Pat declared.

"I've always told you," Dad said to Mom, "I was never meant to grow up."

Mom smiled sweetly. "And you never did."

He drew back cartoon-style, shocked. Then, with a quick check overhead for the mistletoe, he pulled her under it and kissed her. Uncle Fred grabbed Aunt Pat and did the same.

"Oh, Fred!" she protested.

"Mush!" We jumped up and danced around them. "Muchas smooches!" Because there is just something about parents acting all kissy-faced that gets to you. You're happy and embarrassed at the same time. What's a kid to do but holler "Mush!"

Cass's eyes kept darting to her parents, checking how far we could go. "You guys are a bad influence," she told me with a grin.

Freddie and Lucy hung on Mom and Dad's legs. "Smoochy smoochy!"

Still in this clinch, Dad turned and looked down through narrowed eyes, all dignified. "Excuuuuse me, but without mush, you kidlets wouldn't even be here!"

He kissed Mom again. I glanced at Cass and turned away, blushing. He had a point. It's like that teasing song people sing on the playground: "First comes love, then comes marriage, then comes so-and-so with a baby carriage." Silly but true—if it wasn't for all that stuff, this whole family would never have got started!

·18·

Eggplant Pajamas

"You know," I told Cass the next day, "you're not like I thought you'd be at all." We had fallen behind the others at the aquarium's tide pool exhibit.

"So what were you expecting?" she said.

"Well, I guess I thought you'd be like that picture you sent. Where you're wearing that pink dress?"

"Oh, that," she said, tossing her braid. "That's sort of a joke around our house. The dress was totally my mother's idea."

"And you didn't fight her on it?"

She shrugged. "Why bother?"

"You didn't feel . . . like you weren't being true to yourself?"

"Robby! It was just a picture. No big deal."

The trip to the new aquarium in Newport was just one of the special things we got our cousins in on during the vacation days before Christmas. We baked more goodies, like we always do, and took in a Christmas movie matinee.

When Mom had her special reception at the art gallery, Dad took us by so we could see all of her paintings hung up at once. "A short, controlled visit," Mom and Dad kept promising each other beforehand. Sometimes these galleries have pottery sitting on pedestals and stuff, not a good place for three-year-olds to run loose.

But Lucy and Freddie behaved themselves. Maybe, like me, they were a little bit awed. I mean, there was our mom, but she was smiling at us as if from a distance, making me feel almost shy. But proud, too, to see her looking so pretty in her long, swirly skirt, chatting with all the people. Everyone was really admiring her paintings. Cass went nuts over them. The neatest part of all was when we saw my school counselor, Mrs. Van Gent, and she was buying Mom's picture of the little red schoolhouse where all the kids are rutabagas and turnips.

"Well, Robby," Dad said as we got back in the van, "it looks like Christmas might be cheerier than we thought at our house this year. Did you notice how many of Mom's paintings had 'sold' tags?"

And of course it wouldn't be Christmas without a drive around the Douglas Bay Pepsi-Cola bottling plant, where the local owner sets up a lighted display of cutout figures—everything from Jesus in the manger to Rudolph the Red-Nosed Reindeer and a Teenage Mutant Ninja Turtle. We all headed over there on Sunday night. It doesn't take long to drive the loop, so Dad always does it more than once. Four times this year, in fact, because Dad said Freddie and Lucy were the perfect age for it and couldn't seem to get enough.

"Honestly," Mom said, "it seems like we were just doing this the other day. Was that way *last* Christmas? The year's gone by so fast."

Don't grown-ups have a strange sense of time? Christmas doesn't come around nearly fast enough for me.

We went to the early family service on Christmas Eve, the one where the minister makes a point of saying it's okay if the little guys get squirrely. Also he always welcomes all the people who come only on Christmas. He acts like that's okay, he's just glad to see the place so full.

As usual, the story of Jesus' birth in the stable was acted out by some kids. It was neat, with the candles, and all of us singing the songs everyone knows. Only the littlest babies fussed. Even Freddie and Lucy were impressed and solemn.

The minister closed with a prayer for peace on earth. He prayed especially for the children who were hungry and trying to survive wars, and named the countries where that was going on right this minute. It was a shock, in a way, like he was bringing the TV news right into church. But it did have a way of making Christmas seem real and right now and not just an old story about something that happened a long time ago in a far-off place.

Well, I know that a prayer can't fix everything, but I will say this: sitting in that church full of people, there was a comfort in sending my prayer up along with everyone else's. With my eyes shut tight, I could almost feel it rising, one big wish for peace just lifting up from every heart.

The wind buffeted the minivan as we drove home around Tillicum Head. By the time Cameron and I were tucked into bed up in my loft, the rain was beating hard on the roof just over our heads.

"I like that sound," I said. It's extra loud up there, because the ceiling of the dormer's slanted, with no attic space above it.

"Yeah." Cameron snuggled down. "But I was wishing for snow."

Now that's a wish I'd pretty much given up on. Sometimes for Christmas it'd be cold and clear here, sparkly with stars and frost, making our house and woods look like a glittered greeting card. But this weather—wet and way too warm for snow—was what we usually got.

Christmas Eve is the one night we leave the outside lights on—for Santa, you know. Staring up at the colored twinkling lights shining through my rain-streaked half-circle window, I listened to the murmuring of the grown-ups down below, the lashing rain, and, after a while, the even breathing that told me Cameron had slipped off.

But I couldn't fall asleep. Too many things on my mind.

After the grown-ups had gone to bed and Cass went for her endless turn in the shower, I climbed down, dragging my quilt, to see if cookies and milk might help.

Maybe Dad had the same idea, because I found him peering into the refrigerator. He was wearing the flannel pajamas Mom got him for his birthday, the ones especially for gardeners, printed with eggplants, asparagus, and radishes. I'd seen them enough that I'd finally stopped laughing out loud, but they still made me grin.

"Having trouble sleeping?" he said.

I nodded, wrapping my quilt around my shoulders.

He held up the milk. "Want to join me?"

"Sure."

I eased up onto the stool by the counter and watched him take down the glasses and a tin of cookies.

"Dad?" I whispered. "I've got to tell you something." If I was going to get in trouble, I wanted it over with.

Dad set the milk bottle down. "What is it?"

"Well . . . remember when you guys went to town and left me alone a couple weeks ago?"

"Yeah . . ."

I winced. "I did something bad. Not the worst thing, I guess, but pretty bad."

"You did!" Now he had that Concerned Look.

I nodded, staring at the floor. "I . . . well, I opened all my presents. Then I wrapped them back up again."

"You did!" He said this more in surprise than as a question. "Huh." He poured two glasses of milk. "Why'd you do that?"

I blinked. I'd been bracing to catch it for doing it in the first place, not working up an explanation why.

"Well, first I was worried, you know, about Uncle Fred and Aunt Pat's present—that it would be something awful. And by the way, it *is*. I mean, why would people buy somebody pink and green shorts?"

"Hey. You're asking that of a guy in eggplant pajamas? Maybe you should be asking your mother that question!"

I had to smile. "Yeah, well, at least your pajamas are goofy in the right way for you." I took a cookie. "Anyway, after that first package, I got curious about a couple more. And then I just plain got carried away."

"Hmm." He leaned against the counter.

I peered up at him. "Aren't you even mad?"

He thought for a moment. "No. I guess what I am is disappointed."

"Disappointed?"

"Well, yeah. I mean, one of the fun parts of Christmas for us is watching you guys opening your gifts and being surprised. Now you won't be."

Boy, I hadn't even thought about the possibility of spoiling something for somebody else.

"Gee. I don't want Mom to be disappointed."

"So—plan on giving a very convincing performance tomorrow morning."

I nodded, hanging my head. "And you won't tell her?"

"Nah. I don't think there'd be much point in that. Not for a long time, anyway. Maybe when you're grown up—it'll be a good story then." He smiled. "Of course, that's assuming you turn out okay and this isn't the first incident in a life of crime."

"Dad! It's not funny. I've been feeling really guilty."

"Oh, come on, Robby." He gave my shoulder a

play punch. "If this is the worst thing you ever do . . ."

"Well, it's not like I'm two years old anymore and didn't know better. Sometimes it seems like I haven't grown up at all."

"Oh, Robby, of course you have."

"But things just aren't turning out like I wanted. I mean, I wanted Mom to . . . you know, be real happy with me."

"What makes you think she's not?"

"Well, I guess she was happy enough about the play . . ."

"Happy we survived it, anyway."

"But that felt sort of . . . like I was just doing what she wanted me to do."

"We know that, Robby. Actually, Mom feels bad she pressured you into it."

"She does?"

"Sure. She honestly thought you'd like it, though." Dad shrugged. "Grown-ups make mistakes too."

"So she's not mad I never want to be an actor?"

"Oh, for Pete's sake! We want you to be whatever you want to be. Don't you know we think you're a great kid just the way you are?"

Well, this is the kind of thing you like to hear, but you don't have a clue what to answer. So I just sat there enjoying the good feeling of it as the bulbs in the hanging brass lights dimmed and flickered. The wind was rattling the cedar shakes.

"Quite a blow tonight," Dad said.

I nodded, picking another cookie out of the tin, one of Lucy's reindeer. She glops on the frosting like nobody's business.

Then I followed Dad out to sit by the Christmas tree.

The truth is, I feel too big now and shy sometimes to just start hugging my dad, but when he put his arm around me as we sat there, I didn't fight it. I gave in to the nice feeling of my cheek resting against his soft, eggplant flannel pajama top.

With all the other lights off, our faces were bathed only in the colored lights of our huge, fresh-smelling tree, the twinkling of our special ornaments.

Almost like he knew what I was thinking, Dad said, "Presents aren't really the most important part of Christmas anyway."

I nodded. There has to be more to it than presents, I'd decided. If it was just presents, it would be . . . I don't know, *hollow*.

"This looks cozy." It was Mom, her curly hair back-lit by the hall light. "Can I get in on it?"

"Sure," Dad said. "Come on."

Outside, it was stormy, but inside, I sat between my mother and my father in this pool of light and warmth. Christmas Eve all over Nekomah Creek, I thought. Christmas Eve all over the world.

Of course, some people weren't paying any attention. It wasn't a holiday for them.

But that was okay too.

Whatever they celebrated, whatever they believed in, I was just hoping they were having a good night. A quiet night. In our forest homes and way beyond, I was hoping there were lots of places like this. Places in every country, places we never heard about on the evening news, little pockets of peace.

·:19:·

For Joy!

In the morning, I looked out my loft window to a gray world. The storm was over. Small tree branches and fir needles littered the yard.

But it was Christmas! I peered down through the loft slats. The tree was ringed with the heap of presents that knocks me out every single year.

"Cass!" I called down to the lump on the fold-out sofa. "Wake up! It's Christmas!"

I scrambled down and flicked on the tree lights just in time for Freddie and Lucy when they came trotting out. Their eyes got huge. Lucy crowed at the yellow-haired troll doll peeking out the top of her red felt stocking. How had Santa known?

Cameron swung down off the ladder, rubbing his hands together. "Whaddayah say we get going on these presents, huh?"

"Cameron, no! We always have to wait for Mom and Dad."

"Why?"

"They like to watch us."

"Where da snow?" Lucy said, standing on tiptoes at the window, her chin on the sill.

Still wearing the elf shoes, Freddie jingled off to jump on Mom and Dad.

"Get up!" I heard him hollering back in the bedroom. "It's Christmas! Santa came!"

In a little while we had all four parents out in the living room.

"It's hardly even light yet," Dad moaned. "What time *is* it?"

Cameron paced impatiently. "Can we start?"

"Cameron." Aunt Pat gave him a warning look.

Mom said, "Just let us grown-ups get a little bit of caffeine in us, okay? And wouldn't you all like some of my special pastries?"

But we were too excited to eat.

"When I was little," Mom said, "we spent Christmas morning at my grandmother's. We had a huge breakfast and my cousins and I had to wash up every last dish before we could open our presents."

"Cruel and unusual," Dad said. "We never would have stood for that, would we, Fred?"

"Nope," Uncle Fred said. "Poor Mom."

"Gum!" Freddie said. "Santa brought gum in my stocking!"

"Looks like we're starting," Dad said.

The next half hour was the usual once-a-year frenzy of wrapping paper, squeals, and exchanges of thank-yous shouted across the room. Every so often one of the grown-ups would plead for people to slow down or say, "Couldn't we take turns?" But it was no use.

Just as well for me too. "Hey, neat!" I said over and over, trying to act surprised. But what the heck, even if I did already know what I was getting, I liked my presents.

The kids had just about opened everything when Freddie got to the box that held the new bunny I'd bought him. He ripped off the paper, as happy and excited as he'd been for every other gift. But then his face fell.

"Oh," he said, pulling out the rabbit in the blue velvet jacket. "A new bunny." He looked up at me. "Tank you, Robby."

And then he put his finger in his mouth.

My heart sank. Until this moment, he hadn't sucked on his finger for a whole week. I turned to Mom. She met my eyes with one of her Concerned Looks, sad and loving. I looked back.

But then it hit me. She wasn't worried about my little brother—she was worried about me!

"Freddie," she said, "wasn't that sweet of your big brother to think of getting you a nice new bunny?"

Freddie nodded.

With everyone watching me, my face blazed. Sometimes good attention is as embarrassing as bad.

"So, Freddie," I said, wanting to hurry past this moment, "what's the bunny's name?"

"Well, that's Peter," Aunt Pat answered for him. "Isn't that Peter Rabbit?"

Freddie looked at her. He took his finger out of his mouth. "No." He studied the bunny, then he looked up at us. "His name," he announced, "is Bobby Yamaguchi."

"Nice," Dad said, completely straight-faced. "Welcome to Nekomah Creek, Bobby."

Cass handed me a package. "Here's one from us you forgot to open."

"Oh, I guess I didn't see that one." Now I'd have to open those shorts center stage.

My lines ran through my head as I slowly peeled off the paper. *Wow, these are great! Thanks a lot!* Wait a minute. Was this the same paper? I gulped and lifted off the lid . . .

Hey. Paperback books!

"Wow!" I said. "These are great! Thanks a lot! No, I really mean that. But where did these come from? I mean . . ."

"Actually," Cass said, "we were going to give you something else, but after we got here, we saw it wouldn't be right at all."

"Interstellar Pig!" How did you know just which books I wanted?"

She laughed. "Don't you know you're practically famous down at that bookstore in Douglas Bay? The lady told us just what you'd want. She even remembered which ones your parents had already bought you."

"Well, thanks." And I really meant that, too, not just for the books, but for giving me at least one surprise for the day.

Then we got another.

There was a knock on the door. Mom and Dad glanced at each other. People don't show up on our porch out here too often.

I opened the door.

Alfie.

We stared at him. He stared at us.

"I want the boy," he said. "The little one."

Freddie gulped. Mom put her hand on Dad's arm. Dad stood up.

Alfie reached for something under his denim jacket.

I stared at what he'd pulled out. "Freddie, look!"

"Buddy?"

"Freddie," I said, "it really *is* Buddy!" He was probably wondering if I was trying to trick him again. "And look, he's smiling." Where Buddy's face had been loved bare, he now had a newly embroidered pink nose and a red thread grin.

Freddie stepped up and took the bunny. In that moment, while we were all fixed on Freddie's face, Alfie disappeared.

Lucy trotted to the window. She looked out and turned back. "Was dat Santa?"

Freddie's eyes got even bigger. He gazed at Buddy Wabbit and beamed, hugging him tight.

Suddenly Mom and Dad were rushing around, putting together a sack of goodies.

"Run after him, Robby," Mom said.

"Me?"

"You're the only one with your shoes on. Hurry!"

By the time I caught up with Alfie he was out on the road again. I hardly had time to think twice about what I was doing.

"Wait, Mr. . . . Mr. Alfie." I ran around the front of him, huffing a little. "Here's some Christmas treats."

He looked at the sack.

"It's cookies we made. Some pastry my mom only

does at Christmas. Like that. Don't worry. We have plenty because we made extra for the tax man only he wasn't allowed to take it and—oh, well . . ." I was just trying to fill up the quiet, trying to keep him from leaving. Now that he was standing right here, I felt so curious, and like I hated to let him go.

He took the sack. "Thanks." He turned.

"But you don't have to rush off," I said. "You could stay and . . . and visit." Part of me wanted him to, part of me was thinking how . . . well . . . uncomfortable that would be. We didn't have any presents for him or anything. And he sure wasn't much of a talker.

"I'm not into socializing," he said, "but I appreciate the invite."

"Oh. Well, maybe another time." I scratched my shin with my heel. "Uh, I did advertise a reward for returning the bunny—"

"Nope." He put up his hand. "Not necessary."

"Well, if you're sure . . ."

He moved to go.

"So where did you find him?" I said quickly. "The bunny, I mean."

"Oh, he was perched in a bush. Lucky, too. Coulda missed him real easy. Took me a couple days to dry him out, though. Kinda spruce him up."

I fixed on Alfie's hands for a moment, his big hands clutching the goody sack. I pictured them working a needle and thread.

He frowned. "I hope that was okay. Making him look a little happier."

"Oh, yeah. Really. This is just the best thing . . ."

He was almost smiling at me now. Then he winked,

turned, and with that hitching limp, headed on up the road.

Wow. I was breathing hard. This had all happened so fast. I guess you just never know how things are going to turn out.

"Hey, Alfie!" It felt so good to yell.

He stopped and looked back.

"Merry Christmas!"

He nodded, sort of jerky. He raised his hand the same way. Like he was rusty, I thought.

"Merry Christmas," he called, and I knew his voice on the wind wouldn't ever be scary to me again.

Freddie and Lucy were watching me from the window. Freddie was dancing Buddy, making his ears flop back and forth. Looked like the *bons temps* were getting ready to *rouler!*

As I got closer, I could hear Dad's accordion. Wait a minute. That meant he was actually playing for other people! I started to run. This I had to see!

LINDA CREW lives with her husband, Herb, and their children, Miles, Mary, and William, on Wake Robin Farm in Corvallis, Oregon. Her other books are *Nekomah Creek,* which was selected as a Notable Book by the American Library Association, *Someday I'll Laugh About This,* and *Children of the River. Children of the River* won the International Reading Association Children's Book Award for 1990 in the Older Reader Category, was chosen as a Best Book for Young Adults by the American Library Association, and was the 1989 Honor Book for the Golden Kite Award given by the Society of Children's Book Writers.